MW01230543

Copyright © 2020 by Z. F. Sigurdson

All rights reserved.

Published by Z. F. Sigurdson

www.zfsigurdson.com

Edited by Angela C. Hebert

Cover art by Steven Kaul © 2020

Cover design by Chloe Brown © 2020

First Edition: May 2020

ISBN: 978-1-7771362-0-8 (paperback)

ISBN: 978-1-7771362-1-5 (ebook)

This book or any portion thereof may not be reproduced or used in any manner whatsoever without the express written permission of the publisher except for the use of brief quotations in a book review.

This book is a work of fiction. Any and all characters and events portrayed in this book are products of the author's imagination and should not be construed as real. Any resemblance to historic events or figures, living or dead, is coincidental.

THE VEILED SAGAS

BLOODIED

*For anyone who had to dig themselves out of a dark place
and for everyone who helped me do so*

Contents

Foreword

By Z. F. Sigurdson

I don't know where to begin or if I even should.

My name is Zachary Sigurdson, and I am a writer.

Whoof… now that we've gotten that out of the way.

On to the heavy stuff.

After graduating from the University of Manitoba in 2017, I worked what most would call a career, an office job, an adult job. Life as a clerk, a cog in a corporate machine. A place I could make some money until I figured out what I wanted to do with my life. The thing is, the job began to wreck me. Seated at a desk day-in-day-out, my mind wrestling with insecurities and self-loathing. I fell into the worst pit of depression of my life. I went through a breakup. I continued to isolate myself from friends. I drank more, ate worse. A walking shadow when I couldn't feel anything anymore. That went on for over a year. I was not okay. I was lost. I was a walking body unable to take joy in anything.

Through it all, I had two things: a family who was very worried about me and my burning desire to keep writing.

So, in December of 2018, I quit my job and took a sabbatical. With encouragement from my family, who allowed me to work on myself and recover. They were worried about me, and rightfully so. I was not okay. I was what I was always afraid of becoming. "Alone, single, unemployed, and living in my parents' basement." This was literally my nightmare. Nothing scared me more than this. This was how kids would bully me in elementary school. This was everything I was fighting to avoid. This was living my nightmare.

Which is why I was immensely fortunate to find work as an Arts and Culture Reporter at the *Manitoban*, the newspaper of my alma mater. This was the structure that kept me going as I continued to wrestle with my mental health.

Those of you who have experienced deep depression and suicidal thoughts know how destructive it is. You look in the mirror and audibly say, "I hate you. I hate you. I hate you." You convince yourself you don't deserve to be happy. That you don't deserve anything good. You lock yourself away. It's better to be in a hole than in the world. I guilted myself over class, race, and gender, further believing I should just die already. I don't deserve the protection and security allotted by unfair privilege that is denied to so many other people. Why am I here complaining? Shouldn't I be able to handle this? I should just die, but not able to bring myself to hurt my family that way.

Writing and my family got me through this. I forced myself to write every day. I made myself finish my second novel manuscript. I wrote weekly articles. I forced myself into some sort of structure, otherwise I would have plunged further into the pit. February might have been worse than all the previous months combined. I wasn't writing. I felt sick all the time. I was trapped in a basement in the dead of winter.

Suddenly, a bolt of an idea hit me, or rather a rainstorm of a thousand ideas. I couldn't allow myself to begin another full-sized manuscript. I was not okay. I still needed time to heal and recover.

I began writing short stories and novellas with the fury of a man drowning. That's what this collection is. It has the breakneck fear and energy of a man fighting for his own life, because that's what it was. Throughout a lot of this period, I was reading or listening to a lot of vintage science fiction and fantasy. The works of Robert E. Howard, H. G. Wells, H. P. Lovecraft, Edgar Rice Burroughs, and others. While I am the first person to acknowledge their racism and misogyny, I can't help but be enamoured by these works. The sheer lunacy of their creativity, their prose. They wrote with that same energy of a man drowning. Many also struggled with mental health issues that went untreated—in particular, Robert E. Howard, the creator of Conan the Barbarian, committed suicide at the age of 30.

So, with my own writing, I've tried to distill that same energy and hopefully leave out their most unsavoury aspects. I also infused my writing with my love of wider genre fiction; Westerns, Samurai films, Kaiju, Gangsters and Horror movies.

Along with this, I learned from local writers that self-publishing and building a backlog is the key to developing your voice and your niche in the industry. I began working towards building that pile, that foundation that not only helped me develop as a creator, but also the foundation I could use to build myself back up. A literal pile of newspapers, notebooks, and rough drafts.

This is all dark fantasy nonsense mixed, combined, and regurgitated by a demented mind. I write Low and Dark Fantasy. I am deeply tied in the Grimdark aesthetic. These are not the stories of kings and heroes. These are rogues, monster-killers, murderers, and normal people caught in terrible situations. I embrace the lurid, the violent, the bloody, and the savage. My writing expresses how I felt at my darkest points and, paradoxically, how I tried to hold it together. I don't write like this to be edgy. Through writing, I managed to have some semblance of control in my life and over my own mind. In the darkness of violent battles and horrifying monster attacks, I created something to hold on to while everything else seemed to melt away.

Now, I am happy to say I am on the other side of a dark time in my life. I am working two jobs, taking classes, being treated for my issues, and holding a copy of my first genuine published works. It's a mess. It's pulp nonsense, but it's mine and I love it. And I can say, I am okay.

And I hope you can love it too.

I want to thank my family for their endless support, love, and kindness. They have seen me in the pits, my worst days, and they are the only reason I am still around. I love them more than I can begin to describe. Thank you, Mom, Dad, Sarah, Josh, and even Charlie. I love you.

I want to thank Sheldon and Cathy Dyck, Lee and James MacFarland, Nathan Beal and Julia Gamble, Lesley Lindal-Dobson, Phillip Bollman, Divya Negri, Ashley Kowalchuk, and Kelly Huyun; fellow writers and creators Lyndon Radchenka, Emma Skrumeda, Tiffany C. Lewis, Gregory Chomichuk, and Samantha Beiko; and especially my editor, Angela C. Hebert, and my wonderful artists, Steven Kaul and Chloe Brown.

I also want to recognize the many educators that

helped build my foundation when I was a very lost young kid; Randal Payne, Barbra Bell, Lisa Burton, and of course Timothy Beyak, and my brilliant professors at the University of Manitoba; Steven Lecce, Tami Jacoby, Andrea Charron, James Fergusson and Sarah Hannan.

I want to thank the staff at the *Manitoban* for giving me a place to expand my skills and, more importantly, giving me a place to grow and a community to feel loved and appreciated by. Through my work with the *Manitoban*, I've met and talked with many brilliant and fascinating creators, some of which helped me on my path through this project.

I am on the other side of a dark time, and I want to thank everyone who helped me through it.

Thank you.

I hope you enjoy the first collection of *The Veiled Sagas*.

♦

The Veiled Sagas

On the Wrong Side of the Veil, things are different.

Beyond the Veil, through space and time, is a realm undreamt of. A place with the glowing eyes of a sorceress and the quaking wails of titans. The forgotten oaths of failed warlords and double-edged promises of cyberspace. A realm of monsters and magic, of blades and bullets, where kings and heathens rule.

Through the Veil, you have entered the Wrong Side.

Nothing is right anymore.

These are *The Veiled Sagas*.

◆

BLOODIED

It used to all be so normal, thought the stranger. *I used to have a normal life. Now I can barely remember it.* On the Wrong Side, nothing is right anymore. You don't realize how comfortable modernity allows us to be. How centuries of development, industry and cooperation created a world where we can drive to work, order our lunch, and go home to watch TV.

Now life is something very different, she thought. *Now it's a lot darker.* Each day brought new hardships and trials. A world where that progress was scattered, unequal and in constant competition with things beyond our meager comprehension.

The stranger kneeled by the side of the road, scanning for threats. Her alias for the last three weeks: Bryn of Franco.

The forest rose high around her with dark pines and elm trees. The mountains were emerald titans growing in the distance. Forested mountains of what *should* have been the Appalachians. The birds were quiet. The smell of smoke and blood hung in the air. Bryn touched the damage. It was cold.

Off the side of the road was the wreckage of a truck. A 1967 Chevy with a dull sun-bleached chassis. The hood a ruin of warped metal. The doors blown open like an exploded pop can. Bullet holes ripped through the tires.

The wreckage was scorched and blood splattered the interior, but there were no bodies. The side of the Chevy was labelled with *Skerhol Mining Company* and a runic symbol of the local ruling clan.

Bryn circled around the wreckage. Based on the scratches, the truck's cargo box had been full of crates, but they were now gone. She kneeled down, her black cloak falling around her like the folded wings of a crow, and touched a paw print in the grass.

A wolf's paw print.

Bryn licked her lips. She rested her hand on her holster. Her narrow, dark eyes scanned the forest. The trees were silent witnesses to whatever raid had happened here. Bryn was alone.

She kept her hand on her holster as she walked down the forest road. Her sword hung at her hip. A longsword with a bright silver crossguard emblazoned with a pair of wolves leaping from a teardrop.

Whatever happened here, she thought, *it isn't my problem... assuming I can avoid it.* She never could.

She hurried down the forest road.

♦

A rock formation hung over the trail. As if someone had put their hand over for those caught in the famously rainy NeoAnglian springs. In the shadow of the formation grew a small waiting post.

Little more than a shack with a hitching post and trough. The smell of cooking oil drifted from the cracked window. Bryn's stomach growled. Her eyes scanned the area for threats, but she only saw more forest, and that's what worried her.

She adjusted her bag and cloak before marching down the path. Gravel crunched beneath her boots.

The door creaked open. Inside was nothing more than two empty tables and a counter made from a slab of wood and two barrels. A bald little man with an apron sat behind the counter. His round face flanked with black sideburns and bug-eyed spectacles.

"Oh! Good day, miss!" chuckled the little man. "What can I get ya!?'

Bryn pulled up a stool, setting her bag on the floor. She put a couple Canadian bills on the counter. "Whatever I can get for this."

"Oh, excellent!" said the little man. He vanished the money into his apron and busied himself on a propane burner. Food crackled on the hot skillet. "Any money with an Anglo Royal on there works here. I'll tell ya, King or Queen, English or Anglo. All good here. None of them godless Yankee dollars! No, miss!"

He set a musty bottle of beer and a plate of potato and sausage hash on the counter.

"Thank you."

"Oh, it's no problem, miss!" he laughed. "No problem. My mother, you see, she was a good dwarven woman. Always taught me good hospitality is the greatest gift to share. The greatest gift the gods taught men and dwarves. My father, God-fearing Anglo that he was, always said God gave man hands to work. I always wondered how they made it work. Two different peoples. Good people. What brings you this way, miss?'"

Bryn spooned the greasy food into her mouth. It was the best thing she'd eaten in a month. The beer was warm, a bit too hoppy, but it quenched her thirst.

"I'm searching for someone," said Bryn. "They may have come through here a while back."

"Oh, when's about?"

"Five years."

The hybrid, because that's what he was (half-human and half-dwarf), stroked his sideburns. "Don't think my mind reaches that far. Plenty come through here. My mother gave me the steely Dvergr longevity, but my dad died of Alzheimer's a long time ago. Don't think they had the right name for it yet. I don't know how much it will stick."

"They would have carried one of these," said Bryn. She set her scabbard on the counter. The silver wolves on the guard sent chills down the hybrid's spine. He reached forward with trembling hands. His eyes filled his glasses like scopes. He gulped and opened the scabbard by a few inches.

The blade was completely black and utterly unreflective, like chalk.

"Please leave, miss."

Bryn scowled. "No, you tell me. Who carried a sword like this?"

"I don't want any trouble."

"No, you fucking tell me now."

"We're closed," said the Hybrid. "Please leave."

She stared flatly. Sweat beaded across his brow. Her arm shot across the counter, grabbing the hybrid by his collar. She pulled him close. "I bet your mom smacked you for lying, but your dad snuck you sweets and sips of whiskey." He trembled in her calloused hand. "Who were they?! What do you remember?!"

The door swung open and two stout figures entered the shack. Two rangers. Dwarves in quilted tunics with gunbelts hanging with axes. Shields on their backs and steel repeating crossbows slung over their shoulders. The odd spiked steel pauldron or plastic knee pads. One had a thick black beard in a single braid, the other had a short red beard with long hair around his shoulders.

"Hell is going on here?" snapped Black-Beard.

Bryn put the hybrid down. He huffed, brushing himself off. "Greetings, Rangers. The lady was just leaving. I'll cook you up something."

"Thanks, friend."

Bryn glared. She threw back her head and finished her beer. Red-Head had his hand on his holster. Bryn had no interest in a fight right now. She had more information than she previously did. *They had come through here.*

Her scabbard clicked shut, and she gathered her bag. She shoved past the rangers. They were only a head shorter than herself. They glared at her. Passing between dwarves was like passing between forklifts with roaring engines. They were immovable. Stubborn as granite.

The door slammed behind her, and she continued down the trail.

♦

Later that day, Bryn saw the consequences of the raid.

She smelled the bodies before she saw them. A sour, overpowering reek that sent shivers down her spine. She reached the base of another massive shard of bedrock. Across the grey surface was splashed *Traitors. Justice be done* in white paint.

In front of the boulder were sharpened staves. Each crowned with a severed head. Clouds of black flies buzzed in layers over the skin. Birds had already pecked out their eyes.

You could tell they weren't human. They were small, almost child-sized. Their ears were either long or pointed, their noses hooked or squashed. Their skin, being chewed away by the flies, was green. Green like rotten leaves.

Six goblin heads were impaled as an example.

Bryn tried to imagine what their crime might have

been, then she remembered the wreck she found. A truck belonging to a dwergi mining company raided by goblins? That sounded about right.

Bryn carried on. It was getting dark, and she needed to find shelter.

♦

A woman screamed.

The bus was on its side, burning, flames reaching like fingers into the night sky. People screamed, bodies fell. Violence swirled around her. Shadows swam through the chaos. Men in black cloaks. More sharks than men. Pure, bloodthirsty predators. Unreflective black blades snapped like vipers, cutting down innocent people as they fled.

The woman screamed again. It was her own voice.

Bryn snapped out of her nightmare and sat straight up. It was dawn. The grey glow of the day creeped through the forest. She had camped in the nook of a huge oak tree. Her cloak wrapped tightly around her. Beads of dew rolled off her shoulders. She rubbed the exhaustion from her eyes.

Another cold morning on a nameless NeoAnglian road. It must have been almost the end of May if her count was right. Bryn groaned, cracking her back before gathering her belongings.

A gunshot echoed.

Bryn froze. It was a short distance away. She waited for a moment to see if it would continue. It could be another raid on a convoy. It could be a monster attack on a nearby farmstead. Or even a battle. Bandit gangs, goblin clans, isolated settlements, or even dueling Princelings sorting out an insult. Violence bloomed in these mountains like flowers.

A patter of gunfire echoed.

Not my problem, she told herself.

High-pitched screams followed the gunfire.

Bryn bit her lip. Her fingers tapped against her sword's pommel. The gunfire and screams weren't far. Memories played in her head. Memories of her own screams, a burning bus, and incredible violence.

"Oh, fuck me too, right?"

She bolted towards the noise. Her cloak flared around her like raven wings.

♦

Bryn slid behind a rock, her boots skidding on the needle covered ground. The cool pine smell filled the forest. She peered over a rock into a low gully. A shallow stream flanked by boulders. Trees leaned over the gulley like the bars of a cage.

The stream ran with blood. Red-purple blood. A broken body lay in the trickling water.

A goblin runt, no bigger than an eight-year-old child. Its chest crumpled inwards by a crossbow bolt. It wore a ragged denim vest, trousers, and sandals. Its beady black eyes wide and vacant.

The screams and shouts echoed nearby. Bryn crept low and followed the stream.

♦

A collection of stones filled the gulley upstream. The water trickled down the rocks, creating a shallow pool. Cornered in an inlet of the rocks were about fifteen goblin runts. Water up to their ankles. They were trembling and terrified.

Around the gulley were five dwarf rangers. Bryn recognized the two from the outpost. Black-Beard and Red-Head. Three others surrounded the gulley from atop boulders with repeaters aimed at the inlet.

"Please!" howled the only goblin visible. "We don't mean no harm! We don't mean no harm! We were just heading home! We don't mean no harm!"

Black-Beard spat. "Did the ones who attacked our convoy mean no harm!? Did they!?"

"We're just foragers! We don't mean no harm!"

"Bah!" hissed Black-Beard. "You fucking greenies killed them and fed them to your wolves! Then you stole what's ours! Where are the rest of you?! Where is your clan?!"

The goblin, his narrow face barely visible, clenched his jaw. He wore a leather vest over his boney shoulders and a child's MTV shirt as a tunic. His yellow eyes reflected the light within the inlet, like glowing disks. He was trembling.

None of the goblins said a word.

Black-Beard hissed to his compatriot, "Pass me the stick."

Red-Head passed a stick of dynamite. "If you fucking runts don't tell me where your Clan is, we're going to blow you to paste. Do you understand?!

After a long moment the goblin flashed his fangs. "For the WhiteFangs!"

"For the WhiteFangs!" echoed the rest of the runts. Their child-like loyalty to their clan and their brothers held on just enough to keep their terror at bay.

Goblins were always thought to be devious, backstabbing, and cowardly, but no one ever saw a goblin betray another when faced by an enemy. It was the clan against the world. Goblins would murder their brothers, but then die for them in the face of another threat.

Bryn was frozen watching the scene play out. Her eyes never left the terrified goblin runts. They were hidden within the rocks, but it was like watching a pack of children being terrorized. She knew they were *just* goblins, but maybe that was the point. Everyone always said they were just goblins.

All Bryn saw was someone small being tormented. *They're just so small.*

Oh, fuck me twice… She drew her knife.

One ranger stood by a dense collection of bushes. There was a rustle. He glanced over his shoulder but thought nothing of it when he saw a squirrel climbing a nearby elm. He watched as the rangers in the gulley fiddled with a lighter. One stick was more than enough, two was just to see how high their little green bodies would fly. The rangers on the rocks watched like it was a football match.

An arm reached out from a mulberry bush. The razor edge of a knife gleamed in the shadows of the forest. The hand pulled back the dwarf's neck and, before he could scream, the edge was already drawn across his trachea.

The body vanished into the foliage.

A ranger glanced over his shoulder and saw his compatriot missing. "Gregg?! You taking a piss? You're gonna miss the show."

The pair crossed the shallow stream, dropping from their rocks. Repeaters scanning for threats. They didn't notice the silent shadow creeping through the undergrowth. They climbed onto the rock and saw a few drops of blood.

"What in Thorr's name?"

Bryn materialized behind the ranger. Her cloak and cowl transformed her into a reaper. Her black blade raised. The unreflective black metal was invisible in the gloom of the forest.

The other ranger turned too late.

Bryn swung hard, cleaving the ranger in the side of the head. Shattering his dense skull and biting deep into the brain. Bone and blood splattered the boulder.

The remaining ranger yelled. He raised his firearm, but Bryn moved in a blur, slashing the weapon to pieces and impaling the dwarf on her blade. Blood seeped down the tunic.

With his stubborn will to survive, he drew his axe and chopped at Bryn's shoulder. She caught his wrist. He growled, pressing the blade towards her face.

In the gulley, the officers shouted and aimed their crossbows for her. Bryn twisted, turning her opponent. The crossbows twanged and bolts bit into the shield on the ranger's back. Her strength was no match for the dwarf, the axe slowly neared her face. Her arm strained. Sweat beaded across her brow. The edge an inch from her eye. Even as the blood pooled at their feet.

Bryn let go of the sword, leaving it in his stomach, and pulled her pistol. She shoved the chrome barrel under the dwarf's chin. His eyes went wide just before his face disappeared in a spout of blood.

The officers fired more bolts. Red-Head ran across the boulders towards Bryn.

Bryn hugged the corpse, using it as a shield. Bolts rung against the shield. She fired awkwardly at Red-Head. Two bullets ricocheted off the rock. She growled and fired all three remaining bullets. Ribbons of blood sprung from his tunic. His momentum carried him, and he tumbled back into the gulley. His head cracked against a boulder with a wet crunch before he landed in the water. Dead.

In one movement she knocked the faceless ranger into the gulley, drew her sword from his belly and pulled his shield off his back. The body splashed into the gulley, the water growing redder by the second.

Black-Beard watched his party vanish in seconds. He grit his teeth and threw away his crossbow. He shouldered off his shield.

"Come on! Piece of shit human!" he snarled.

Bryn obliged and dropped into the gulley. A cloaked shadow wielding a black-bladed longsword and a gleaming dwarven shield covered in dents from the crossbow bolts. She dropped into a fighting stance.

Black-Beard glared. His beard hung past his chest. He stuck the explosives into the rock above the inlet. The goblins' reflective eyes glowed in the shadows.

"You gonna die for some goblins?"

"Someone is."

He smirked and lit the fuse. The sparks poured over the entrance to the inlet.

"For Skerhol!" screamed Black-Beard, axe in hand.

His boots splashed as he charged shield first like a battering ram. Bryn spun out of the way, dropping low and drawing her blade across his thigh. The blade bit through the padded tunic.

He snarled, spinning on his injured leg. The axe rung on Bryn's shield, vibrations climbing up her shoulder. She swung back. They went back and forth, metal clanging, shields ringing. She stumbled back. As if she had been hit with a sledgehammer. It was like chipping away at a marble statue. He could take more punishment than she ever could.

The fuse sparked, already halfway used.

Bryn swung high, but instead of slashing, she smashed her hilt into his face. He groaned and bashed her with the shield, knocking her off her feet. Cold water soaked her clothes. She raised the shield, the dwarf hammered downwards, like he was chopping wood.

The fuse only had a few seconds left.

Bryn thrust the point of the blade into his other shin. She whipped her sword upwards, slashing him across the cheek. He screamed. Blood dripped into the water.

She sprung off her heels and slashed with the tip of her blade. The edge cut the fuse at the base. It fell into the water, going out with a hiss.

Black-Beard backhanded Bryn with the shield. She fell backwards into the water, her head ringing. When she spun around, Black-Beard slammed his boot on her shield, pinning her sword under it.

"I've seen it all. A human protecting goblins." He raised an axe. "We used to team up against them!"

As he lowered the axe towards Bryn's skull, a green body slammed into Black-Beard. His eyes went wide. A dozen more bodies slammed into him, knocking him off his trembling injured legs and into the water. The pack of goblins howled and cackled. They pinned his limbs, the sheer weight of numbers holding the dwarf down. His terrified voice muffled by the water.

A runt raised a shiv, and the dwarf's gurgling screams were silenced.

The pack of runts immediately swarmed the twitching corpse. Stripping him of anything valuable. The pack scattered like ants and began stripping the other bodies. Boots, weapons, ammunition, belts, buckles, coins, dice, everything. Anything the runts could afford to carry.

The runt, the one who had stood up to the dwarves, stood over Bryn. The size of the child, his comically large ears did nothing to hide the lethal wildness behind his beady eyes.

"Thank you," said the runt. "Thank you. My name is Rac of the WhiteFangs."

Bryn, who was covered in blood, took his tiny clawed hand. "Bryn."

♦

Bryn agreed to help the pack of runts back to their clan. They crept through the trees. The midday light flooded through the forest in beams of yellow and gold. They kept low to the ground, staying in the shadows. Rac said that dwarf rangers were swarming the forests, hunting for goblins. Soon they would find them and exterminate them.

Hours passed and night neared. The golden light grew to burnished copper. An uneasy tension followed the party.

The pack of runts were tired. Their foraging expedition had been during the previous night, which was why they had got caught out in the morning. Bryn crouched low to the ground, the party trailing behind her in the long shadows of the forest.

She froze and held up her hand, halting the party. She heard marching, movement, and shouts in the underbrush.

Bryn waved Rac to follow her as they crawled through the underbrush to investigate. They came to the edge of a rise, hidden beneath a mushroom-lined log and behind tangles of ivy. Bryn pulled back the foliage.

In the distance was a column of dwarves. Beams of light from electric lanterns scanned the underbrush. Fifty bearded warriors, frustrated, and armed to the teeth. Weapons clattered. At the head of the column was an armoured thane barking orders.

Rac and Bryn slunk back and out of view.

"Why are they gunning for you?" asked Bryn.

"Dwergs need reasons to kill goblins?"

"Fair," said Bryn. "But they usually come up with one."

Rac glared. "Fine. The other day, some RedCap raided a convoy from the Skerhol mines. Our bosses executed the traitors, but the dwarves don't care. They found their reason to exterminate us now."

Bryn nodded. "Where is your clan?"

"In the mountains," said Rac, "Grey Canyon is where our clan has been my whole life, now the dwergs want us out."

They slunk away. "How old are you?" asked Bryn.

"Three winters, ma'am." He looked up with the eyes of a wild killer.

She led the party around the column and hurried towards the mountains.

◆

Dusk scattered long shadows across the mountain slope. The party arrived at the entrance of Grey Canyon and the home of the WhiteFangs. The forest opened up to a bare riverbed. They followed the trail to the edge of the forest, where at the crest of a slope rose two huge pillars of stone flanked by jagged cliffs. The entrance of a vast labyrinthine canyon.

The pass was guarded by a squad of goblins. Huddled around a fire in the shadow of the gates. They had repeaters and handguns, all rusted despite their best efforts. At the edge of the firelight was a pile of sleeping wolves. Their hunched shoulders rising and falling.

One wolf's ear perked up. The trees rustled. The wolf

turned its shaggy head and growled. The rest of the pile did the same. Snarling teeth bared.

The goblins' senses were only slightly dimmer than the wolves, but far more acute than any human. They grabbed their weapons and aimed towards the shadows of the forest.

Rac stepped out, a hatchet on his shoulder that looked as big as a battle axe on him. He waved. The goblins lowered their weapons. The rest of the party filtered out of the foliage. Then Bryn followed. Her hood down, sun-kissed face exposed.

A larger goblin with a dishpan helmet painted red stepped forward. A RedCap. A middle ranking goblin. He cocked his head. "Rac?! Is that you?"

"Yeah, boss," said the runt. His sandaled feet padded up the riverbed. Bryn followed. "The human saved us! Saved us from the dwergs!"

The RedCap looked Bryn up and down with reflective eyes. His hooked nose and long chin frowned. Around his neck hung a collection of wolves' teeth. A sabre and pistol stuffed into his belt. The wolves surrounded Bryn, growling.

"What the fuck happened?" sneered the goblin.

Rac told them.

The RedCap looked like he had been slapped in the

face. "Agh! Get out of here! Go help! We're getting out of this canyon at daybreak!"

"The dwarves will be here in two hours," said Bryn.

The goblins looked at the runts, then each other. As terrified as they were furious. The RedCap snapped. "What are you all looking at!? Go! Go help the camp! We're moving out." They scattered. Some leapt onto their wolves, holding on by tufts of grey fur. They bounded off with blurred speed.

"You're coming with me," hissed the RedCap. He looked at her weapons. His eyes narrowed. "I'm going to need those."

"I brought back your runts," said Bryn. "I killed to protect them. I warned you about an oncoming attack. I think some trust is afforded."

"That is for the bosses to decide," said the RedCap. "Please, human, the belt."

She grimaced and handed over her weapons.

◆

Grey Canyon was a maze of trails, ravines, rock formations, and caves. Along the walls of the canyon were tents and hovels for goblins. Midden heaps of bones and refuse, a field smithy ringing out sabres and knives, piles of wolf cubs nursed by their mothers. Wagons and sleds pulled by skeletal mules or goats were being piled with bundled tents and other supplies.

Goblins of all shapes and sizes watched as the RedCap led Bryn. It was a menagerie of gargoyle faces. Wolves prowled between the goblins with hunched backs and bared fangs. One goblin patted a wolf's snout. A pair of warriors carried spears topped with cylindrical explosives with push-pin fuses. Bryn had seen those. Some called them Boomsticks, ThunderSticks, or FireLances. Explosive spears had their uses.

At an intersection of the canyon was a series of switchbacks climbing a corner of the canyon wall. Warriors with torches patrolled the heights. Above was the entrance of a cave with a firelight within.

"Come on," hissed the RedCap. "The bosses will want to speak to you."

Bryn nodded and followed.

The cave was warm and dry. Curtains of patched fabric draped the walls. Rugs and skins scattered around the floor. A banner across one wall with the ferocious jaws of a white wolf.

A pair of goblins hunched around a brazier, ripping strips of meat off a charred flank of deer. Both with grey wolf skins draped over their shoulders, bulking up the crooked creatures with the fanged faces hanging over their heads. Armoured in scraps of metal and stolen pieces.

When they saw the RedCap with Bryn, they rose to their feet. Clawed hands resting on sabres. One goblin had a piggish face and short up-shooting tusks. The other had a long hawkish nose, one eye blind, pale like an orb of milk.

"What is *this* doing here, Finnok?" said Milk-Eye.

RedCap sniffed. "She brought the runts back. They said she killed four dwarves on her own."

"Four?!" said Pig-Face. "The Great Wolves are toying with us today." He rushed forward. His blade tipped towards Bryn's cheek. "Why did you save our runts?"

"A spy probably," said Milk-Eye. His remaining red eye searched Bryn up and down. "How can a *female* do that kind of damage?"

"With this," said Finnok. He dropped her scabbard on a bear skin. The silver wolf crossguard flashed in the flickering firelight.

Milk-Eye's good eye went wide. He crouched by the blade. He touched the wolves and hissed, retracting his hands. "Silver. Bah!"

"The blade," hissed Finnok.

With a delicate hand, Milk-Eye drew the black blade from the hilt. The long bar of black metal refused to shine or reflect the fire. The edge bitten and gouged in places from fighting. Milk-Eye dropped it like it was a snake. He hissed. "Get rid of her!"

Pig-Face smiled with his pointed tusks, his blade inches from Bryn's throat. She grit her teeth, trying to figure out a way to get her sword back and escape from the middle of a goblin infested canyon.

"Bring her…" rasped a voice like a creaking door hinge.

Bryn hadn't noticed the cot in the far corner. In a nest of blankets was the most ancient goblin Bryn had ever seen. Most goblins didn't live past forty. Life expectancy was incredibly low as it was.

This one was ancient. His sagging face like a vulture's beak. Fingers like knotted roots on skeletal arms. His robes of patched fabric stained red, layers of wolf teeth necklaces around his neck. His sickly green skin splotched with patches of white.

He raised a yellowed claw. "Come closer, human."

Bryn eyed the goblins before kneeling at the side of his cot. He smelled like an old book. He was like a part of the wall of fabric and skins. The banner hung above him, as if the Great Wolf Gods were watching over him. He coughed. "You have done us a kindness never done by a human." He coughed. "Why?"

"I don't know," said Bryn, after a moment she decided on an answer. "I saw unnecessary cruelty."

The elder goblin cracked a smile, in his blackened gums remained only a few sharp teeth. "I trust you know how desperate we are. Dwarves on our doorstep. We are vulnerable."

"I am sorry to hear that," said Bryn. *But that's not my fucking problem.*

The elder's eyes floated to the sword on the ground. He bid the RedCap hand him the blade. He took the sword in his skeletal hands, taking care to avoid the silver crossguard ornamentations. "Evil men carry these blades."

"I know what kind of men carry these blades," said Bryn. "I am searching for them. What do you know of them?"

"I know they are evil, and I know they have not been seen in these lands for several years. You are better to search south."

Bryn nodded. "Thank you. I'll take my sword and be off then."

"Please," rasped the elder. "I am old, stranger. I am old, and I am weak. I have no strength to battle dwarves anymore. My tribe is too few. Our wolves are too hungry. We cannot survive this attack."

"Then leave," said Bryn.

"We will," said the elder. "But we've lost so much to the dwarves of Skerhol. So much. Our remaining warriors are scouting our route out of these mountains. We will head west. We will join the realm of the Goblin King under the Rokki Mountains. We didn't expect this response so quickly."

"Then you're all fucking fools," said Bryn.

The goblins snarled, but the elder hissed them into silence. He fell into ragged coughing.

"She is not wrong," he finally said. "We should have left the moment our own kin committed that crime. We thought justice would mean something, but it didn't. Only blood has worth here."

"None of this is my problem," said Bryn.

"No. It's not, and yet you saved our younglings, our runts. Too young or too small to survive on their own." None of this meant anything to Bryn. None of it. She had her own journey. She wanted to slap the Elder for his chirping. She needed to leave. Leave before the canyon was awash in blood.

"You have seen the black heart of men, human," said the elder.

"Yes," hissed Bryn.

"Will you not spare us the same fate as you have shared? Must we all suffer the same? Must we? You showed kindness to our young, but you'd only delayed the inevitable." He frowned, his eyes glistened. "Will you leave them to that fate again? It would have been better that they died this morning."

Bryn glared at the decrepit creature.

"I only ask for my clan. My brothers."

He handed her the sword. It felt especially heavy in her hands. "What do you want me to do…" she said, feeling almost defeated, knowing what was about to come.

"Hold them. Fight them. Give us our chance to flee."

"I am just one person."

The elder chuckled before falling into more ragged coughing. "You lie to yourself, human. You are much more than you give yourself credit. I can see it in your eyes." He leaned forward on his frail arms. The goblins rushed forward, concerned. He snapped at them. "I am not dead yet, you fools. Human, I can see in your eyes the fire. A fire that burns hotter and longer than the stars. You are unconquerable. Your journey will be long. I see it. As clear as I see you before me now."

"I'm guessing you probably need glasses," said Bryn.

"Ha!" More coughing. "And a wildness too. Your journey will have far harder opponents than a regiment of dwarves. Give us this boon, and the gods will remember."

"I'd rather have cash."

The elder cackled again. "We can spare you weapons and ammunition. Little else."

Bryn looked into his dulled eyes. His brow as wrinkled and lined as cracked clay. His eyes like orbs of blood. Swirling and gleaming in the crackling firelight. She saw the reflections of the concerned goblins. The terror in their eyes. The fear of extermination. Of genocide. The WhiteFangs would vanish and never be worth remembering.

"Fine," said Bryn.

♦

Night had cast the forested mountains in a dark blue. The moon was hidden by encroaching clouds. Thunder rumbled in the distance. The ribbons of black clouds spread across the sky.

The regiment of dwerg rangers, fifty strong, marched towards the gates of the Grey Canyon. Their shields and weapons rattled; their boots crunched the soil; their lanterns creaked on their handles. The thane at the head of the column raised a gloved fist. Their boots clattered to a stop. Several rangers raised their crossbows and firearms, all aimed at the solitary figure standing between the pillars of stone.

Her cloak flapped in the growing wind. The taste of a strong storm was coming in.

"Is that a human?" hissed one lieutenant.

"Aye," said the thane. "One that's sided with the greenies." They had found the bodies of their warriors. They could tell it wasn't any goblin that had killed them. He raised his axe. "Get her!"

The figure vanished as the first few bolts and bullets ricocheted off the rock. She evaporated into the darkness of the canyon.

"Charge!" roared the thane. "Let's get some goblins! For Skerhol! For Clan Austinn!"

"Clan Austinn!" roared the regiment.

The warriors charged up the slope, their boots shaking the ground. They roared their war cries. The column evaporated into rabble with their thirst for revenge. The thane, with his winged helmet and gleaming axe, led his warriors from the front.

Images of glorious revenge flooded his mind; goblins on spikes and wolfskin cloaks. He charged through the stone gates and entered the canyon to find… nothing. The canyon was empty. The long, jagged walls were bare. A few empty fire pits and midden heaps remained.

There was a clatter of pebbles. The cloaked figure stood atop a boulder. She raised a spear in hand. A spear with no point, only a can-shaped head. Before the thane could bark an order, she lobbed the weapon.

It struck a ranger in the chest and exploded, engulfing three others in fire and shrapnel. Dwarves screamed and scattered.

"Get in line! Get in line!" roared the thane, trying to organize his forces pouring into the canyon. "Shoot her!"

She had already vanished as bullets rung off the stone. A shadow dashed between rocks. Metal flashed and another lance slammed into the rangers. Two more vanished in the explosion. A cauterized limb fell at the thane's foot. The smell of burnt hair stung his nose.

"Am I leading a bunch of yearlings?!" he roared. "Spread out!"

The regiment was still swarming into the canyon. They were bunched up, confused, and excited. The shadow appeared between two rocks. Repeaters fired, but she was already gone. The thane drew his revolver, tracking her movement. She leapt between rocks, launching another lance. Dwarves screamed as three more evaporated in fire and shrapnel.

The thane fired. His bullet glanced off her shoulder as she tumbled behind a rock. The thane and a squad of warriors rushed behind the boulders only to find a trail of blood.

The thane and several warriors followed it for a dozen yards. The rest of the regiment spread out, searching the canyon for the WhiteFang goblins.

A ranger kneeled at the end of the trail of blood. "She's gone, sir."

"Find her!"

The ranger stood up and something clicked. Fire and rock burst from the side of the canyon, swallowing two more rangers. The thane dove out of the way, debris ringing off his armour.

"Find her! She's stalling for the fucking goblins! Find her!"

♦

Bryn bit down on the fabric and pulled it tight. The bullet had left a gash on her shoulder. The rangers were flooding the canyon. A racket of heavy boots and jiggling weapons. She looked up at the sky. The inky cloud cover rumbled.

Lightning struck a distant peak. The wall of rain barreled towards the canyon. Bryn drew her revolver and pulled one of three small shrapnel grenades from a midden heap. She breathed. There was a shuffle nearby.

Across the canyon was her next weapon cache. She pulled the pin on the grenade, holding the lever tight. Timing her throw.

The wall of rain, like a tumbling mist, rolled towards her. She closed her eyes. The water slammed into her like a wall of pellets. Her shoulders already grew heavy. The lanterns of the rangers glowed through the darkness. Shouts and curses at the weather sounded nearby.

Bryn exhaled and bolted.

She lobbed the grenade at the feet of the rangers. It exploded in a pillar of dust and debris. Repeaters crackled, bolts flew past her. Bryn slapped the hammer of her revolver, firing into the dwarves. Two more fell to the ground.

She dove behind a boulder as bullets ripped into the cover. Shouts told her they were about to surround her position. She tossed another grenade around the corner. An explosion and screams followed.

Grenades were good, they rolled and had a timer. The Boomsticks were also good. They were accurate and had a pressure pin.

She flicked the revolver open, reloaded and snapped it shut. In another midden was a repeater with a strap of ammunition. Along the wall of the canyon was a trail leading around the corner at the first split in the canyon.

Rain pattered the stone. Thunder roared overhead.

Bryn threw the strap over her head. She pulled the pin on the last grenade and dropped it at her feet.

She dashed for the trail, bolts flying past her shoulders. The explosion knocked the boulder on its side. It rolled down the canyon, injuring several more rangers, taking them out of the fight. It crashed into the gates, blocking the exit.

Bryn's cloak flared behind her, a bolt went straight through the fabric and flew past her side.

She dove behind the corner of the trail. The path hugged the jagged cliff like a winding snake. It rose high above the canyon floor. The rain had begun to flood the rocky channels. The heavy footfalls of the dwarves following her close behind.

Bryn vaulted over a boulder, taking cover and cocking the lever of the repeater. She narrowed her eyes, peering down the long barrel of the firearm. Shouts and stomping boots echoed just behind the corner. The rain pelted the cowl of her cloak.

The first dwarf to come running around the corner was young; barely grown out his red beard, his cheeks smooth and rosy. His blue eyes were lost in reckless fury. He wore a red scarf around his neck. Around one arm hung a handkerchief. A gift from some girl, probably.

Bryn exhaled and fired.

♦

The rangers were pinned by the cloaked warrior. Bodies had piled at the corner of the trail. The rangers, using their own friends for cover, were unable to dislodge her. Twice they attacked with a shell of shields, but she always found the gaps. The trail was filled with bleeding and groaning bodies.

"What do we do?!" asked a blonde-bearded ranger. His face covered in soot and blood from tending the injured.

The thane, watching from the bottom of the trail, narrowed his eyes. "Send a squad. Find a way around."

The blonde-bearded ranger nodded. "What are we going to do?"

"Wait for her to run out of ammo." The canyon was filling with water. His boots were soaked. Water ran off the pauldrons of his armour. "It's just a matter of time."

♦

Bryn thumbed the last three rounds into the magazine of the repeater. She stood up from her cover and slowly backed down the trail.

"She's running!" cried a voice.

Bryn fired. The dwarf's head jerked back with a spout of blood. Three more dwarves rushed forward, hobbling over their dead comrades.

"ValHal!" they screamed.

Oh, I'll send you all there.

Bryn followed the path towards a bridge that crossed the canyon that had become a roaring river. Lightning webbed across the sky. Dashing from cover to cover, she fired.

Bryn dove away from the gunfire. She swore as she reloaded her revolver with the last six rounds. She was almost in position. The dwarf numbers reduced by half. *They still haven't broken and run.* They were either as stubbornly brave as the stories told, or just twice as dense.

She fired around a corner. A ranger's knee burst, and he tumbled off the bridge of stone, vanishing into the roaring currents below.

She saw the thane leading his men, roaring encouragement and threats. Bryn narrowed her eyes and fired. The shot knocked him to the ground.

◆

The thane's head was ringing. He tore off his helmet. The bullet had ricocheted off the helm and tore off the wing decoration. He was bleeding above his eye.

"Sir!" barked a lieutenant. "Sir!"

"I'm alright! I'm alright!" said the thane, rubbing his head. He was all right. He saw the shadow of the cloaked warrior dash from boulder to boulder, sparing time only for a desperate shot from a handgun. Each shot killed a dwarf warrior with pinpoint accuracy.

Where is that squad?! Thought the thane. "We need to corner her."

♦

Bryn ran down the trail, water falling all around her. She slipped, catching herself on a rock as debris fell into the raging waters below. She looked up. She was near a split in the canyon, the trail snaking between the rock wall, and a triangle-shaped formation hanging over the growing river below.

She reached the last weapon cache. A bow and a quiver of arrows from a crevasse. She had one bullet left in her revolver. She threw the weapons over her head and kept running. Lightning flashed. Blood trickled down her arm from her shoulder.

She turned a corner and yelped. A crossbow snapped.

Bryn was knocked onto her back. A bolt sticking out of her side. Blood gushing through her flannel shirt. She yanked it out. Her hand trembling. A squad of rangers drove up the path towards her. She kicked herself backwards and fired her last shot.

A warrior died. Bolts flew past her head. She hissed and hobbled back up the path. She stopped; the rest of the rangers were flooding in from that way. There were around twenty left. She ducked as bullets and bolts crackled against the rock around her.

With blood running down her leg, she climbed the triangle-shaped stone formation. She ducked behind a shard of rock and knocked an arrow. The dwarves drove towards her position. She winced, pain exploding through her side. Her chest muscles stretching, arms bulging, she drew the bow to full length and loosed.

A dwarf fell into the raging currents below.

Pain seemed to overwhelm her senses. Her vision red. She fired another arrow, striking a dwarf in the throat. And another, and another. Each arrow knocking them back. The battle was as clear to her as a map. Each time a dwarf tried to get in position to fire back, she loosed another arrow.

The dwarves huddled behind cover. She could see the thane at a loss for words. How could one human woman fight against them? Who was this woman? Who had trained her? Where did she come from?!

You have no idea, asshole. She fired and caught him in the chest. Knocking him to the ground.

She ducked back behind cover and smiled through the pain. She reached into the quiver. Her smile dropped when she felt nothing. Her eyes dashed around searching for options.

"Fuck me…" she hissed under her breath. "Hey! You guys still want to do this? Cause I can do this all day!"

The dwarves paused. Unsure of what they were even fighting for anymore. So many of their friends and brothers lay dead. The thane groaned, rising to his feet, using his axe as a crutch. The arrow hadn't dug deep enough.

"Surrender, human!"

"Try again!" shouted Bryn. "I'll let you all walk away! You can all go back to your miserable little lives digging up gems and fucking bearded women!"

The remaining rangers shared looks. Unsure if the violence was worth the effort anymore. What was revenge when there was none of them left? The goblins were long gone. What would they be leaving Skerhol with?

"You got a minute!"

The thane glared at his warriors. Rain pattered his

cheeks and ran down his beard. His blue eyes focused on the shards of rock where the cloaked warrior was hidden. She had cost him so many of his clansmen.

His face dropped. "She's bluffing! She's out of ammo!"

Boots clattered up slope.

"Fuck," said Bryn. "It was worth a try."

She drew her sword. Water splashing off the chalky black blade. She held it in front of her face, shoving back the memories of the men who carried them. It was a tool to her. A painful memento, but also a tool.

How the hell am I getting out of this?

Her mind wandered for a second. Reaching into her training. She sheathed the blade and rubbed her hands together.

She could hear her master's voice on the wind. His stern, unforgiving scowl. For five years since her Exposure, she had lived in a monastery of lost monks. Refugees from long ago who had made a home in the abandoned *Chateau de Jean*. They had explained the new world she had entered, fed her, trained her, and let her become one of them for five years. They called her Sister Rong.

Her master had to be compelled to train her. And train her hard he did.

She could picture him now. A small Shaolin man with a perfectly bald head that glowed like brass in the sunlight. His deeply lined and perpetually frowning face was as hard and immovable as rock. The nine pale dots sparkled on his brow.

"Again."

The battle on the cliffs fell away and she was atop the hills with her master. Foothills of the Laurentian Mountains in South Franco. The golden grass rippled in the breeze. The Franco countryside was always beautiful, scattered with birch and emerald pines.

Rong couldn't enjoy it. With the monks she was always restless. She always looked to the mountains to the north or the river basin to the south. Endless miles of dense pines and grassy glades. The constant itch to leave and begin her search across this new and terrifying world.

This darker, more brutal, plane of existence, filled with monsters and magic. Every storybook and mythological text come to life. The modern world, her world, bled slowly into this incomprehensible realm creating chaos in its divergent developmental timeline.

She needed to leave. To search for the men who carried the black-bladed swords.

Master turned, his gnarled knuckles around his reed staff. "Again."

"We've done this every day for a week."

"And each day you failed."

"No! The last two days I managed!"

His brown eyes, disappointed shining beetles. "Barely. Again."

He turned to look out over the mountains. His saffron robes billowing in the wind.

Rong saw a branch discarded in the grass. She licked her lips, her brown eyes watching her master. She picked up the stick, eyes unmoving. She charged on silent steps, she swung.

Flowing like water, he evaded the strike. With his eyes closed, he flipped Rong onto her back and pinned her to the ground in a single movement. The reed staff snapped and gave her a fresh red welt on her cheek.

She grit her teeth and reluctantly tapped out.

Without a word, Master let her go. He resumed his position looking out into the distance.

Rong sighed. A wide flat stone sat in the grass, rubbed smooth by decades of training. She spread her hands across its surface. She exhaled, allowing her mind to clear and her body to relax. Her weight shifted to her hands, and she slowly raised her legs, bringing them together until she held a perfect handstand. Before long, her muscles strained and sweat dripped down her face. She would only break the position at Master's orders.

Most days he would leave and return hours later. He always knew when she was slacking.

The grass rippled like the waves of the ocean, the breeze cooled her face. A falcon flew overhead. Dust and seeds spiraled overhead in the wind.

Bryn blinked. She wasn't Rong anymore. She was Bryn. She was another stranger caught up in the violence of this world. She gripped her blade. *They have no idea who I am? Allow me to give them a demonstration.* She retreated from the pain in her side, letting her instincts take control. Her higher self cast aside for the violence to come.

The rangers jumped to either side of the rock, weapons out, but there was no one there. The survivors of the regiment crept across the outcrop like armoured beetles. The thane tore the arrow from his chest. Axe in hand, he peered over the precipice towards the raging waters below.

"She jumped?" asked a warrior.

"I…"

There was a scraping of rocks. The thane turned just in time to see the woman leap onto the outcropping from below. She had scaled the slick, rocky cliffs with bare hands. She roared, drawing her blade from its sheath and across a ranger's throat in a single elegant motion.

The body dropped at Bryn's feet. She hissed, her cowl blowing back onto her shoulders, revealing a beautiful sun-kissed face, pointed chin and narrow brown eyes. Her long black braid whipping behind her back, wind lashing at her face. She was no longer herself. Bryn was lost in the motion and charged the dwarf rangers. Their numbers didn't matter anymore.

She was a hurricane of motion. The sword flashed in devastating arcs. Droplets of blood and rainwater flew off her chalky black sword. She hissed like a mountain cat as her sword bit into the dwarven tunics, padded armour, and metal bracers. The sword snapped like a viper, breaking crossbows and weapons.

A weapon cocked. Bryn drove the blade into a dwarf's foot and threw him off balance into another ranger. They tumbled, screaming, off the edge of the precipice. She swam through their ranks, they were unable to draw their axes in time, and when they did, she flowed around them and drove her blade through their vitals.

Blood splattered her face. She snarled. She lobbed off a hand holding an axe and, before it could hit the ground, smashed it into a ranger's face. The body crumpled to the ground. Bryn was drenched in blood. Dark crimson rolled off her boots and down the rock in ribbons.

The final three stood above her. The thane and two of his lieutenants. They were squat hunched forms. The rain pattered their armour and lightning illuminated their grim faces.

The thane gripped a two-handed axe. He had joined the fray and retreated back after Bryn hammered him with her sword. His pauldrons were dented, breastplate gouged.

Bryn raised her blade. "What's your name?"

"Rire Rikkson," said the thane.

"You're going to die, Rikkson."

"We'll see," he said. "Get her!"

The lieutenants rushed forward with shields and axes. They tried to overwhelm her with sheer force, like tanks driving down a hill. It was a very slick hill, however. Bryn kicked up a discarded axe and leapt into them.

In a swimming motion, she diverted both their blades. She used their momentum against them, using the hook of their axe or the pommel of her sword to knock them off balance. In the instant they realized they had made a mistake; she had already slashed open their throats.

Rikkson rushed forward as his friends' bodies collapsed against the rock.

Bryn countered. She floated around his guard, drove the point of her blade between the plates of his armour. Blood gushed from his shoulder and side. He roared and backhanded her.

Pain spread across her face. She stumbled backwards. Rikkson roared and stormed forward. She barely managed to keep her footing when he swung. She diverted his blade into the ground.

Rikkson slammed the butt of the axe haft into her chest. She gasped and swung low.

He caught her weapon on the haft of the axe. With a sharp yank, he used the beard of the axe like a hook. The sword spun away and clattered down towards the trail. The silver hilt glinted with a flash of lightning.

The thane grinned at his small victory, just long enough for the stranger to smash her fist straight into his face.

Pain shot up her arm. It felt like punching a wall. Rikkson, wide-eyed, looked more surprised than anything.

Bryn changed tactics and smashed the heel of her hand into his face. His nose broke with a sharp snap; more blood poured down his face. She tried to kick out his legs; again, it was impossible. Dwarves were built like panzers made of marble. They broke before they bent.

Rikkson chuckled through the blood and swatted the

stranger in the stomach with the butt of his axe. The force sent her sliding down the slope clutching her side. The pain pierced through her mental walls. She pushed herself up.

When she opened her eyes, Rikkson threw the haft of the axe over her head and began choking her with it. Her voice cracked.

The thane laughed in her ears. His tobacco-stained breath whispered, "You will never leave this place, girl. You will be forgotten. No one will ever know you existed. You're dead. You're nothing."

She gasped something.

"What was that, girl?"

She grit her teeth and wrapped her fingers around the haft of the axe. "You don't know a damn thing about me."

In a blur of movement, she twisted and slammed her elbow into the thane's face. He grunted and let go. With one hand on the axe, she twisted it out of his hand. Launching off her piston-like legs, she leapt into the air, axe in hand. A heavy backwards kick slammed into Rikkson's chest. The sure-footed dwarf tumbled down the formation.

Bryn landed almost catlike. Her form was perfect, despite the blinding pain.

Rikkson groaned as he gathered himself up. His black-bearded jaw hung open with his shock. His eye grew a huge, purple welt. "Who are you?"

Bryn moved from her Horse Stance and transitioned into an aggressive Bow and Arrow stance. Palm forward and fist ready to strike. "No one."

Rikkson roared, charging forward with a dagger. "ValHal!—"

Bryn swept the axe horizontally in a perfect arc. The bearded head tumbled off the outcrop and was swallowed by the flooded canyon.

Lightning webbed across the black sky. Bryn was a tiny bloodied silhouette surrounded by bodies. The rocky outcropping like a diamond over the rushing water dripped with blood. Ribbons of red falling into the river.

The woman fell to her knees. Her body vibrating. She let out a blood-curdling howl. Fists clenched at her sides. A long, feral scream, more terrifying than the storm. She had been slashed in a dozen places, her side still screaming with pain. She screamed, releasing all her hate for this new dark world.

She had won.

Tomorrow would be the same.

That's what happens when you become Exposed to the Wrong Side. Every day is a fight.

BEACHCOMBER

The screen door clanged open. Geoff stepped into his childhood home for the first time in two years. The carpet was still stained, and the walls still reeked of cigarette smoke. The TV buzzed in the corner.

"Who the fuck is there?" drawled a deeply unpleasant voice.

Shudders climbed Geoff's spine.

Feet clattered down the stairs. Geoff's little brother froze midway down. Olly was almost twelve. Geoff was eighteen now. Olly's ruddy little face was covered with acne. His hand-me-down clothes hung off his thin frame. His wrist was purple, even though he tried to hide it with his sleeve.

"Holy shit! Holy shit!" said Olly. "Dad! Dad! It's Geoff!"

Olly leapt the rest of the stairs and slammed into Geoff. Geoff hugged his brother hard, feeling like it had been a lifetime. *Christ, he's thin. Was he always this little?* Geoff had sworn he would never return to this place, but he always knew he had left one thing behind.

There was a shuffle of feet and Dad stood in the doorway of the kitchen. He teetered on his feet, his face flushed tomato red. *Already? It's only eleven in the morning!* Geoff glared at his father. His father glared back. Geoff and his father were both of the same thick and strong build from time on the ocean.

Geoff leaned down and whispered in his brother's ear, "Go grab your things. Just like we always talked about."

Olly's body shuddered. He looked up, his eyes wide and consumed with fear and confusion. He didn't believe it was finally happening. He couldn't believe it was real.

"Come on," said Geoff. "Give us a sec."

Olly nodded and went back up the stairs, sparing a second to glance over his shoulder.

Geoff and his Dad stared at each other for a long time. The years of hate and fear had built up and exploded many times. So many times… Geoff had left at sixteen. He had saved every penny, he had worked his fingers to the bone as a fisherman. He would continue working as a fisherman. Now he was able to change things for Olly.

"What the fuck do you think you're doing?" hissed his father.

Geoff reached into his jeans and pulled out a folded slip of paper. He held it out. His father snatched it, his half-drunk eyes scanning the words like how scholars read ancient Greek. His mouth trembled with the ribbon of smoke from his cigarette rising past his bulbous head.

"I've come for my little brother," said Geoff, matter-of-factly.

"No, you fucking can't!" roared their father. "Not in my house!"

"The lawyer disagrees. I can't bring you up on charges, but I sure as hell can take my brother away from here."

"No, you can't!"

"Yes," said Geoff, snatching the paper back. "I can. I have an apartment in town. I make a good income. As far as the lawyer's care, I am going to be Olly's guardian."

There was a clatter and Olly stood at the top of the stairs with three overstuffed duffle bags hanging off his shoulders. His face grimaced like he smelled something wrong.

Geoff gave his brother an assuring smile. "Come on, Olly. Let's get out of here."

"Not a fucking chance!" roared their dad. He stuck a finger in Geoff's face. "You can't do this to me, boy. Or I'll—"

"You'll what?!" hissed Geoff.

Dad was frozen, his round ruddy face flecked with silver hair. His teeth stained yellow. Geoff called the old man's bluff. He was a miserable drunk and an abusive piece of shit. Geoff wasn't a chubby little kid anymore. He was a wide-shouldered fisherman with hands like power tools. Olly would walk out of here.

"Come on, Olly," said Geoff. "Let's get out of here."

"Don't you fucking move!"

Geoff stared flatly. He held out a hand for Olly. "Pass me one of those."

After a painfully long silence, Olly crept down the stairs. He handed Geoff one of his bags.

"You can't!"

Olly threw on his shoes and walked out the door. Geoff turned and they headed into the greenhouse at the front of the house.

"Leave! Fine, you little shits! Your mother—"

Geoff whipped around and punched his father in the jaw. The man crumpled against the doorframe. Shock coloured his face. It hadn't been much of a punch, but that was the point. It was enough to shut him up. He had made the mistake of mentioning their mother.

Geoff adjusted his bag. "We'll see you on the court day. My lawyer will be in contact."

Geoff wrapped an arm around his brother and led him to his truck. Geoff's body vibrated with adrenaline. He was already driving away from the house and towards town. If Geoff had the money, they would leave this fucking place. For now, his small apartment was all they had. It was enough. Anything was better than that place.

"Is this real?" chirped Olly.

"It is now."

The Karlson brothers shared a smile and headed towards their new future.

♦

Six Years Later.

The thunder rumbled in the distance. The Pier Inn was crowded with a usual collection of unhappy locals huddling over their beers and bowls of chowder. The radio hummed along with "For What It's Worth" by Buffalo Springfield. No one spoke.

The waitress collected empty bottles and half-eaten

plates. There wasn't any laughter. There was no game on. Donna, the overweight motherly innkeeper, leaned against the bar reading a magazine.

Everyone just stared at their food.

"This storm's taken the warmth right out my bones," said Old Man Ralf.

A few fishermen nodded. One, a Mr. Alec Jonas, grumbled, "Something's not right. I have never seen a Labour Day weekend this empty and pathetic."

"It'll pass," said Beatrix, the general store manager. She threw back her head to finish her beer. "All things do."

Alec scoffed. "It's been four bad seasons in a row. Eleven if you don't count the shark attack that brought every thrill-seeking dumbass with something to prove."

Old Man Ralf shivered. "I don't mean that, boy."

"I'm thirty-two, Ralf," said Alec.

"Don't matter. Somethin's not right about that storm rolling in. I feel it right here." He tapped his chest. "We'd best be careful."

Another fisherman, Bruce Keller, turned. "Boats will be fine, you old coot. One storm is the least of our troubles. Now we got the Jefferson's Diner closing down. Last month it was Lonny's Shop." One of the Jefferson boys was sitting at the bar, looking ashamed scooping stew into his mouth.

"We're cursed," said Alec Jonas. "City folks left us behind... fucking liberals got us by the balls... before long the illegals will be taking over..."

"Will you just shut up, Alec," hissed Beatrix. "You're as insufferable as ever."

"Just speaking the truth."

"You know what's true?" She opened another beer. "You're an asshole. No wonder Maria left ya for the big city."

Alec got on his feet. "Fuck you!"

"What?!" snapped Beatrix, challenging the fisherman.

Alec's lips curled like he was trying to think of something clever.

In the corner table sat the Karlson brothers, Geoff and Olly. Black hair and grey eyes, like every other Karlson since the town's founding. Olly watched as Beatrix spat back and forth with the fisherman.

"Don't pay them any mind," said Geoff, not looking up from his newspaper.

"You think they're fucking?" asked Olly. "Only people doing the nasty argue that much."

Geoff shook his head, he grimaced at the Business and Politics section. Everything was a shit show, whether it was here or anywhere else. "No. He's just an asshole, and she's just stubborn. Can't argue with stupid, it just feeds their ego."

Olly nodded and returned to staring at his stew.

Geoff glanced up from the disappointing current events. *He's thinking again,* thought Geoff. "What is it?"

Olly didn't say anything. He retreated into himself. Geoff's now eighteen-year-old little brother was more perceptive than anyone gave him credit for. *He'll be the one to escape here. That's for sure.* His scholarship was his ticket out. Not Geoff, no sir. Geoff had already accepted his lot in life to be the fisherman, just like his dad had been. Just like Papa Karlson had been. Just as Great Grandpapa Karlson had been. And all the other Karlsons. At least one fisherman a generation to keep their name in the industry. *Or what was left of the industry.*

Geoff pushed the newspaper aside. "You give any thought to what you're going to major in?"

Olly shook his head. "Mom wanted me to be a doctor or a lawyer or something really flush like that."

"And then you will fly to Mars on a pig named Gerome and sing 'The Sound of Music'…"

Olly poked at his stew. "I don't have the grades for that anyways…"

"No," said Geoff. "You're smarter and more astute than half the rich kids that get into those programs. You'd just be fucking miserable trying to be a doctor or lawyer, and doubly miserable being one. What do *you* want to do?"

Olly shrugged. His face was pale and narrow, barely a wisp of facial hair. His acne had scarred him something fierce. His nose was moon-like in texture.

"Don't think about what Dad said or what Mom would have wanted. What do *you* want to do for the rest of your life?"

"I don't know. We don't have the money for me to fuck around in school for half a decade. The scholarship will only go so far."

"Do you want to teach? You'd be good at that."

Olly shook his head. "Any fishmonger's wife can be a schoolteacher. Besides, I won't babysit someone else's brats."

"Academic? Teach university level."

"No prof jobs. Economy for that is dead. No one values full-time professors anymore."

Geoff tapped the newspaper. "And we're all the stupider for it."

"Do you want to write? Maybe go to film school, try to be some big fancy screenwriter or something?"

Olly shook his head, but it was clearly more of a reflex than an actual refusal.

Geoff leaned back and sipped his beer. He was bigger than Olly, especially across the chest and shoulders. Working on the docks and on the water since he was thirteen would do that. Geoff's hands and face were worn like old leather, even though he was only twenty-four.

Olly poked at his stew some more, it was getting cold. "I haven't seen enough of the world to know what I like and don't like. I just don't want to waste mine or anyone else's time."

"Finding a better life will not waste *anyone's* time."

There was a long silence before Olly nodded.

"Do you really want to end up like them?" Geoff pointed subtly at Alec and the other miserable fishermen. The world had left them behind one way or another. Geoff refused to let the same thing happen to Olly.

Olly frowned.

"Didn't think so. Eat up, I don't want to be caught out

there when the storm *really* hits."

The gusts of wind sputtered against the roof of the inn. The windows tapped with the initial waves of rain. Thunder roared in the distance. The storm was going to be a bad one. Geoff knew it. He hoped it would pass without too much destruction.

Geoff took a long sip of his beer.

"What the hell are you looking at, Karlson?!" barked Alec Jonas.

Geoff put down his beer. Olly had stared too long.

Alec had already crossed the room and was standing over Olly, who retreated further into himself by staring down at his food. Alec huffed, his square chin covered in whiskers. "You think you're so smart and fancy with that big city ticket out of here? You think you're better than me?!"

"Sit. Down. Alec," said Geoff, who looked up at the older fisherman.

"Oh, now we got the big brother. I don't like you, Geoff Karlson. You're too smart for your own good. Always got your nose in a book."

"And you always got your mouth opening and closing," said Geoff. *Seriously? I have to deal with this douche enough already.* Alec was a constant thorn in everyone's side. An angry man who wouldn't be happy if a gold-titted mermaid fell into his boat.

Bruce Keller stood up. "Leave the kid alone, Alec."

"Nah, I want this little shit—" he pointed at Olly, but kept his glare aimed at Geoff, who rested his head on his fist, bored of the argument already, "—to know that once he leaves, he ain't fucking welcome back here. He ain't one of us."

"You the one going to enforce that?"

Alec and Geoff kept their eyes locked. A silence overtook the entire inn. Olly glanced back and forth between the two. Geoff didn't move a muscle. He didn't even blink.

The entire room rumbled with the next thunderclap.

Geoff gripped his beer bottle. His entire body wound up like a spring ready to explode into action.

Before anyone else could say anything, the lights went out. Everyone groaned. "Not again! Third time this month!" moaned Donna.

Lightning flashed outside, followed immediately by the thunder. The storm had arrived. The rain hammered the roof and glass as if marbles were being pelted at the inn.

Something is *wrong*, thought Geoff. He could see the shadow of Old Man Ralf fidgeting violently across the bar. He felt it too. The storm rolled in quickly, which was not uncommon, but something was off. Geoff stood up, ignoring Alec Jonas.

Geoff sniffed the air. There was something there. Something rotten.

The lightning illuminated the window. Geoff's eyes went wide. There stood a single shadow… Tall and crooked, with yellow eyes reflected in the low light.

Everyone froze.

"What the—" started Donna.

The window screen exploded in a cascade of shattered glass. Rain and wind stole the warmth from the room. Lightning struck again. Light illuminated more shadows at the windows.

"Everyone get out!" yelled Geoff.

It was too late.

In the flashing light, shadows burst through the windows. Huge bent figures with yellow eyes. Panic ensued. The shadows tackled fishermen and patrons to the ground. Screams were followed by wet snapping sounds, like the crack of a wet towel.

Donna screamed.

Geoff felt for Olly's arm and hauled his brother out of his seat. A silhouette stood jerking the kitchen door handle. More lightning revealed Beatrix's face twisted in complete terror. Geoff raised his leg.

"Move!" He brought a hard kick down on the door. The adrenaline pumping through his body. The door slammed open, the lock breaking into pieces.

"Everyone go!" Geoff ushered a handful of people through, Olly and Beatrix first.

Geoff turned at the last second. He saw one of the creatures step through the window. Its crooked shadow lingered over one of the bodies. The crumpled form of Old Man Ralf whimpered. The shadow picked him up by the throat. Lifting the old fisherman off his feet. His thin wrinkled face ran with tears. Blood dripping from a claw mark across his cavernous forehead.

Lightning cracked.

A pair of jaws opened. Long translucent needle teeth spread with long strings of saliva. The smell of low tide filled the room. One piercing eye saw Geoff. A yellow eye of pure feral hate.

Geoff slammed the door shut. His heart pounded in his chest. He tried to lock the door but realized he had broken it. Beatrix ran forward and lodged a chair under the door handle. Heavy fists slammed into the door. Screams were cut short. *How many of them had I'd known since childhood?* Thought Geoff in horror.

"That ain't gonna hold," said Geoff.

"Then let's get out of here, Karlson!"

There were five of them. Geoff, Olly, and Beatrix were followed by Alec Jonas and Bruce Keller. Geoff rolled his eyes as the two fishermen stood trembling, staring at the door. Something slammed the door again and Alec yelped.

The group ran out the back door and into the gravel alley. Rain poured down hard. Geoff felt the cold-water soak through his coat and shirt immediately. His boots were waterproof, but Olly's weren't. Geoff hugged the back wall of the inn. He could hear screaming between the claps of thunder.

Geoff peered around the corner. More crooked shadows dashed between buildings. Across the way was the Chinese restaurant called Wan's. Screaming erupted from within the Wan's apartment. Geoff's stomach dropped. *They have two daughters.* He peered around more. The shadows moved into every building with blurring speed. They shrieked and hissed with an incomprehensible feral joy.

"What is it?" whispered Olly.

Geoff narrowed his eyes. He could see the frothing ocean in the harbor. Between two docks came more shadows. Each wave revealing more crooked figures. A single bent figure sat squat atop a huge rock along the shore. It leaned on a huge greenish-silver trident.

"Geoff, we got to go."

Geoff didn't move. The boats in the harbour bumped against one another and the dock. The canvas was stored and ropes tied. A pair of boats lurched to the side. Followed by the next pair. Then the next. All the boats in a line lurched as if…

A shadow began to grow out of the water. A single massive shadow.

"Run," hissed Geoff.

They nodded and followed him without question. More screams and cries erupted throughout the town. Shadows crashed through windows, lights flickered. The group of survivors ran down the alley only to pause at the corner near the boarded-up ice cream shop.

"What are we gonna do?" asked Olly.

"My truck is by the store," said Beatrix. Her general store was only a block away.

"We need to tell everyone," said Alec. "We need to raise the alarm."

"What about Dad?" said Olly to Geoff.

Let them take him, thought Geoff. Though he couldn't very well let that happen. Dad was at the edge of town in the old Karlson house. It would be difficult on foot.

Beatrix scoffed at Alec.

"You think I'm gonna run?" hissed Alec, as he glanced around the corner.

"You want to fight those things?" scoffed Beatrix. "None of us even know what's going on!"

"I can, and I will. Don't you got a shotgun in your shop?"

Beatrix nodded. Her wet chestnut hair hung around her shoulders. "And a .45 under the counter."

"Jesus," said Geoff.

"What? After those kids stood up the gas station last year."

Alec scoffed. "Kids? Those fucking—"

"We got to go," said Geoff. "Olly, you go with them. Get out of here. I'll go get Dad. He has his double-barrel and plenty of tools in the shed. Once I get those, I'll be fine. Keller?"

The shaking fisherman looked up.

"I need you to raise the alarm along the south end of town. I'll head north." *Up to Dad's.*

"You're going to run there?!" said Olly.

"Yeah," said Geoff.

Keller nodded and took a look around the corner. His hands shook. "I'll be back. I promise." He took one last look before running around the corner.

"You're crazy," said Beatrix.

"Yeah," said Geoff, taking another look before his turn. He took a deep breath. Sparing one last look at his little brother. He remembered when Olly was seven and found a frog. Dad had knocked the frog out of his hand before calling him a queer. *Fucking old man.* Olly was the good one. Olly was the one who needed to escape. He was the one with the future.

Geoff sprinted down the main strip. Years prior it would have been packed with tourists. People laughing, families with ice cream, and couples kissing. Businesses and shops busy and prosperous. Now half the strip was boarded up, windows shattered, and clearance sale signs discarded.

Geoff ran past the old diner. *One more block. Then left.* His legs burned. He needed to go faster but couldn't risk slipping. He blinked away the rain peppering his face. Lightning erupted across the black sky.

He turned at the intersection, holding on to the stop sign while his feet slid across the slicked asphalt. There were a few empty houses before the forest north of town. At the end of the long dark road was the old Karlson house.

His feet left the ground. His back slammed on the rough ground. The back of his head throbbed. He groaned. "Fucking hell..." Geoff opened his eyes. The falling rain stung his cheeks. "Goddammit."

Thunder crashed around him. He tried to move but couldn't. He could feel the rumble in his chest. His clothes were completely soaked. He felt another crash in his chest, but it wasn't thunder. It was followed by another, then another, and another. He looked up, the intersection upside down in his vision.

He saw a huge shadow strut across the intersection. Each long, segmented leg taking precise steps forward. A huge barnacle-pocked shell hovered six feet above the ground. Long, twitching antennae searched cars and boarded-up shops. A pair of immense claws, the size of canoes, snapped periodically. It halted at a blue Volkswagen Beetle, the antennae twitching with excitement. A pair of green periscope eyes rose from the great shell's shadow.

One huge claw reached under the Volkswagen and tossed it into the abandoned pet store. The crash was silent with storm raging around them.

A tiny quivering form stood up from where the Volkswagen had been. *Bruce Keller.* He raised his hands to rub his eyes. Geoff rolled over to see. *He must have doubled back to find a hiding spot. Coward.* Neither of them could believe what they were seeing.

The shadow of the shelled monster raised one claw and brought it down right onto where Bruce stood. He vanished. When it removed its shell, there was nothing but a crater in the asphalt.

Geoff stumbled to his feet, stepping backwards slowly. *I have to run. I have to get Dad.* He didn't turn to see if the creature pursued or even noticed him. He ran as hard as he could. Rain pattered his face. He passed the dense trees at the edge of town. He kept running. It was almost six miles to the old Karlson place.

♦

Geoff's lungs burned and water stung his face. He felt like he was drowning. His legs were numb with lactic acid. His jeans chafed and sloshed. Shadows flashed against the blue luminance of the lightning strikes.

He could see a light in the distance.

He turned the corner around the waystone he had passed countless times before. The old oak tree that he and Olly had both broken arms trying to climb. He stepped onto the gravel drive. That old grey pickup stood broken and unused as it had for the decade before. The old Karlson place had a greenhouse entrance. Thin walls of wire mesh with wicker furniture. The light was on in Dad's upstairs room.

Geoff winced as he opened the door. It felt haunted. Everywhere had a bad memory. Dad had no sense of privacy when it came to disciplining them. A Christmas or birthday without a beating wasn't something Geoff understood until he moved out into town.

He dripped on the coffee-stained carpet of the entrance. The many fishing and hunting trophies brought too many memories. That dull reek of mothballs and those cheap cigarettes that Dad loved made a scar on his temple ache. *Why am I even here?* The old man didn't need or deserve a rescue. Old Patrick Karlson was a piece of shit that Geoff would enjoy watching get ripped to shreds by those creatures.

Geoff went to the fireplace. Above the mantle was Beauty. A beastly looking double-barrel shotgun. Its worn wooden stock polished shiny from hundreds of hunts. He gripped the heavy weapon and went to the broom closet for the ammunition boxes. *If Dad is anything, he is consistent.* He took Dad's old leather shoulder bag and filled it to the brim with shells.

Geoff heard a creak.

He jumped to the side as Patrick Karlson swung his razor-sharp Bowie knife. He must have thought Geoff was an intruder.

"Dad! It's me!" Geoff jumped back. Dad overswung, leaving him off balance. Geoff rushed forward to lock his dad's arm, pinning him against the wall. "You son of a bitch! It's me."

Patrick Karlson's eyes focused. He relaxed. He still had his old strength. His round wrinkled face held his perpetual frown. He shoved Geoff away.

Patrick was wearing a housecoat and slippers. "What are you doing here?" he hissed.

"Hello to you too, Dad."

"What do you want? And what the fuck are you doing with Beauty?"

"We got to get out of here," said Geoff. "Something bad is happening."

"I ain't going anywhere, boy. What the fuck you really doing here? Needed a damn gun? Fine, take her. Enjoy. Give her a blowjob while you're at it, paint the ceiling. More use than you'll ever do."

"Jesus Christ," hissed Geoff, picking up the bag of

ammo. "I come here for ten seconds and you already prove that you're the biggest piece of shit a guy could ask for. Now, get dressed. We got to go."

"I told ya. I ain't going anywhere."

"Be stubborn old man. It'll kill you."

"Disappointment is the real killer. You. Olly. Your mother."

Geoff was about ready to knock the old man on his ass when another clap of thunder shook the house. The light from the windows illuminated the taxidermy around the room. Snarling boars and terrified deer all staring at Geoff.

Geoff growled, shoving his anger to the side. "I ran here from town because something is *wrong*. I know you don't believe me, but something attacked the inn."

"Probably just some freaks from the city. They got all sorts of quee—"

"It had teeth six inches long! There are things coming out of the ocean! We got to get out of here."

Old Man Karlson did something he never did. He laughed. "Jesus, you smoking that powder again? You tripping balls? That's what the kids say?" He laughed again. It was sickening to Geoff. Patrick Karlson only laughed when he was causing pain or insulting something or someone.

Another crack of lightning. It felt very close.

"Fine! Stay here and die! I only came here because Olly asked me to."

Dad laughed again. "Don't you wave that little queer in front of me like—"

Patrick hit the ground hard, the knife clattered against the tile near the kitchen. Geoff's knuckles stung. He loomed over his father, shotgun at his side. "Never talk about my brother like that. Got it?"

Patrick spat a glob of blood on the carpet. He didn't say a word. No snarky comment or threat. Just his perpetual glare. Suddenly they were back six years, when Geoff took Olly away. One way or another, the Karlson men spoke with their knuckles.

Another crack of lightning. This time right over their heads. There was no delay in the thunderclap. It felt like an explosion going off right next to Geoff's head. He hit the floor and covered his ears. The light and sound stung him right to his brain. After a few seconds, the ringing went away.

"Jesus Christ," said Dad.

Geoff opened his eyes.

Patrick Karlson stood by the window, staring. Geoff

joined him. Outside, the old oak was shattered in half, bloomed out like a mushroom. Embers and wood chips were scattered around the yard. Flames began to lick up the broken branches. A single torch in the storm, leaving long shadows dancing across the front yard.

Figures stood in the yard, tall and crooked. Yellow eyes reflecting the smoking firelight. There were at least five of them in the yard, all either crouched low or standing straight like a soldier. Geoff knew that more were coming out of the woods.

One stood by the garage. It placed a hand on the old pick up. In one hand it clutched a trident. Its yellow eyes went from the vehicle to the window.

"We gotta go."

"I ain't going anywhere," said Dad.

"You gotta be—"

"Listen, wise-ass. I appreciate you coming to get me, but I'll just slow you down." He crossed the room to the table by the front door. He tossed Geoff a pair of keys. "I fixed the old Harley. Get out of here."

Geoff held out Beauty.

Dad laughed again. Geoff almost laughed. *A lot of freak occurrences today.* He opened up the bench against the wall in the landing. The old man groaned as he got to one knee to reach in. He produced a Winchester Repeater and a bandolier of ammo. Then he brought out a double-sided boarding axe, like the ones used on an old ship. "I'll be fine. Now get the fuck out of here. Use the old trail."

Geoff nodded and went to the backdoor that led into the garage. He looked back at his father who loaded the repeater. Geoff had no words for the old man.

"Dad?"

"Hmmm?"

"Go to hell."

"Ha! I'll see you there, worthless sperm."

Geoff slammed the door. He exhaled. "Nope. I won't miss him." Geoff had always imagined it would end with one of them killing each other or Geoff just putting the old man in the hospital. It almost felt unfair that those monsters got to have a go at him. Geoff smiled. *He could live with that, though.* He had to get back to help Olly.

He waited for the first gunshots before opening the garage. It was the old family project. Well, Dad's project. He started the Harley and rode out and around the back of the house. He didn't watch the burning oak tree or the creatures that tried to follow. He especially ignored the gunshots and breaking glass.

He headed for the old trails he had explored his entire

life. Water sprayed his face. He could barely see as he rode through the dense trees that flew by in a blur. The headlight flashed against the birch trunks. He tried not to think about Dad. A lifetime of abuse flashed in his mind. He knew he would never see him again. *The abuse will never be paid for. Patrick was gone now.*

It was more a reluctant acceptance than anything.

He pushed the Harley faster through the trail. Mud splattered Geoff's jeans and arms. He couldn't stop. He headed the long way through the woods until he arrived at the trail running parallel to the highway.

The Harley bucked as he climbed the ditch. On the properly smoothed asphalt, he swerved. Geoff let out a breath. He glanced back at the highway. He could escape and get help. He could get help. *No.* He had to make sure Olly was safe. He had to help them now. The storm would make the journey too dangerous. He had to do something with what he had on hand.

He revved the engine before heading back towards town.

♦

The storm raged heavy over the town. Lightning flashed every couple of seconds, thunder rolled continuously, and Geoff was riding towards it.

As he neared the town, he saw something he hadn't seen

in years. The old lighthouse in Miller Park was illuminated. Its rotating spotlight spinning like a giant signal lamp. The lighthouse was the highest ground in the area. Located at the edge of a cliff and surrounded by dense birch trees of the park. One of the usual tourist attractions. *When we had tourists.*

He accelerated towards the lighthouse.

He had to get Olly out of town. *He can't stay. He's the one with a future.* Geoff would fight for the town. For his home. He was never going to go anywhere anyways. He grimaced at the wind stinging his cheeks. *I can die here.* He had already expected to, just not so soon.

He followed a low stone wall at the edge of the park. He swerved into one of the gravel trails through the trees. He could hear gunfire and shouts nearby. The top of the illuminated lighthouse was visible through the trees. He was so close. He reached for Beauty slung over his shoulder.

Geoff swerved around a waystone. A figure stood in the center of the trail. Geoff wasn't able to swerve to the side. It came so fast. It leapt onto the front of the motorcycle. All he could see were claws trying to rake across his face. Feral dripping teeth swallowed his view. He shoved Beauty forward into the mouth.

"Fuck you!"

He pulled the trigger.

Beauty kicked, and the creature's head was blown off clean. Geoff's ears rang. As the slimy body fell, its claws raked down Geoff's arm. Razors slashed into his forearm. He growled as he felt the hot blood flow down his wrist. He held on tight and turned the final corner before the clearing surrounding the lighthouse.

The area was flat and clear, but the grassy meadow had been reduced to mush. He felt the wheels buck and bump over something. In the mirror, he saw a single clawed hand sticking limp out of the mud.

The Harley's wheels kicked and sputtered. The ground was too muddy. The Harley halted, chomping at the dirt. Geoff got off and looked up at the lighthouse. An old brick and plaster tower topped with a metal and glass cap. The beam cast out into the infinite darkness. A pair of people were up in the tower with rifles. The brick building at the base of the tower was boarded up and barricaded with boxes and crates. The entire museum built into lighthouse was now surrounded by a makeshift wall. Beyond the lighthouse was the ocean. The storm raged above. The cliffs frothed with the torrent of saltwater below.

"Geoff! Geoff Karlson!" shouted a voice. Lightning cracked, and Geoff could see the dozens of heads behind the wall, cowering. Silvery barrels of rifles and firearms poked out.

Geoff gripped Beauty and hurried forward. An old settler's cart moved aside, and he entered what almost looked like a World War I trench with ragged, mud-covered townsfolk armed with anything they could find.

A body slammed into Geoff, the pain in his arm stung. Beatrix hugged him.

"Thank God you're okay!" She had a shotgun on her back. He could feel the bulge of her revolver in the front of her pants. She was caked in mud.

Alec Jonas leaned on a bolt-action rifle. "We thought you were a goner."

"Where's Olly?"

Beatrix and Alec looked at each other.

"Where's my brother?!"

"We don't know," said Beatrix.

"What happened?" said Geoff. He overlooked the crowd. Most of the town was here. Fathers, mothers, sons, and daughters. The weird mixed extended family that always made up a small town.

He glanced over the shoulder of John Wan, the Chinese restaurateur. His pale face was scrunched up in wild rage. Inside the mill were the surviving children and elderly of the town. A few people were injured and being tended.

One old man, Jimmy Bloer, sat on a stool with a knife, whittling posts into stakes. The Emerson daughters, three blonde girls of sixteen, were handing out granola bars and bandages from a wicker basket.

"We got as many out as we could," said Alec. "Those *things,* they ransacked everything. They chased whatever moved. That fucking crab thing tore through every building that turned a light on. They're fucking animals."

Geoff gazed through all the people here. He knew them all, but there were many missing. Everyone had lost someone over the last few hours. Everyone.

He glared at Alec. "And you guys thought it was a good idea to turn the fucking lighthouse on?!"

"We got to high ground with everything we could. We needed a way to tell everyone where to come." said Beatrix. "We tried to get a vehicle, but we couldn't leave everyone behind. Olly, the mayor, and a few others... We were about—"

"They're coming!" shouted a voice. Someone was at the top of the mill's tower with a rifle. The crack of the firearm was followed by shrieking from the forest line. Geoff glanced over the crates. Hundreds of pairs of glowing yellow eyes hovered in the darkness of the treeline.

A few rifles cracked. Townsfolk with shotguns waited for the creatures to approach closer, but they didn't. The glowing eyes remained motionless.

Geoff reloaded Beauty, he looked at Beatrix. "Where's my brother?"

"We need to get the children and elderly out of here," said Beatrix. "Olly went with the mayor, and a few others tried to get the bus sitting at the school and bring it to the base of the hill, but they never came back."

"They're dead," growled Alec between launching .303 bullets into the trees.

Geoff gripped Beauty, holding himself back from shooting Alec himself. *No way. Olly is too smart for that.* "They'll be back. I know it, but we can't wait for them to save us."

"No," said Beatrix. "We can't. But we can't get out of here. The park is flooded with those things. They got us under siege. This is a fucking fairy tale nightmare."

"They're just dumb animals!" said Alec.

"Even animals can hunt," said Beatrix. "We need to get out of here. We can't escape through the park, they have us cornered there. Then we got the goddamn cliffs".

Geoff met Beatrix's eyes. "We can probably get down the cliff. Most of us have jumped off of it one time or another."

"The elderly can't do that!" barked another nearby townsfolk, a Kaley Brayersen. She loaded bullets into magazines and clips. Her red hair pulled back with a blue bandana.

"If enough of us attack at once," said Alec while reloading, "we could probably break through and get to the school bus."

"But we don't know how many there are," said Beatrix.

Geoff rubbed his chin. "We can't go over the cliffs. We can't go into the woods. We don't know anything about them. We don't know how many. And they haven't brought their big monster. If we stay, we are all dead. If we try to fight, dead. Try to escape, dead." *There has to be a way.*

"Why the fuck are they just standing there?!" barked Alec. He fired again. The bullets vanished into the trees.

Geoff stood up. The rain pattered against his broad chest. He looked into the hovering pairs of eyes. A few fell from the gunfire, but they were quickly replaced. Lightning cracked. In the trees were what seemed like hundreds of hunched figures. Fins and spines along their bent backs. Geoff squeezed Beauty's stock. "They are waiting."

"Shit," said Beatrix.

Geoff ran through the Museum, passed the huddled children and elderly. He exited through the back door of the Lighthouse. He stood over the precipice of the cliffs. Jagged rocks and violent tides frothing and writhing. Memories of summer days flashed in his mind standing in the same spot.

Lightning flashed. Along the jagged cliffs were shadows scaling the rocks. Dozens of the deep-sea creatures. Pairs of feral yellow eyes stared up at him.

Beatrix ran up beside him. "Oh, fucking shit."

"Like fish in a barrel." Geoff raised Beauty. He pulled the trigger and blew off the head of the nearest creature. Its body fell back into the water in a cascade of its own black blood. A handful of people who joined them fired downward into the water. Shredding the screeching creatures. Their bodies plunking into the foamy surf.

"This is too easy," said Beatrix.

Geoff loaded Beauty with a flick of the wrist. "What do you mean?"

"They send a group to climb up here, but the others aren't attacking."

"Yeah," said Geoff. Thinking about what he would do on one of those old hunts with Dad. He fired Beauty again, cutting a creature in half. His eyes went wide. Thunder crashed, but between the thunderclaps, he heard other crashes. "No! This is the distraction." He pointed at some of the townsfolk firing. "A few of you stay. We're being jerked around!"

They ran back through the lighthouse. People shrieked. Geoff needed to get them out. *I have to get Olly out.* There has to be a way. They had to find a way. There was always a way.

What if there isn't?

Geoff slid into a spot behind the barricade. The horde still hadn't moved, but the crashes continued. Birch trees swayed in the distance.

What if there is no way out?

The yellow eyes separated down the middle.

What if no matter how hard we fight, we inevitably lose?

The trees parted in the middle. Birch trees broken in half. Lightning flashed and an immense shadow stepped into the clearing. The gunfire stopped. Everyone gawked at the monster. Its two large claws snapped periodically, its long antennae twitching and searching.

A single, crooked figure stepped out into the muddy clearing. It leaned on a trident. Its feral eyes focused. It limped up to the leg of the crab monster and patted it lovingly.

"God help us," said Alec.

"I don't think he can hear us anymore."

Geoff reloaded Beauty with a snap. "We have to get them out of here."

"How?"

Geoff looked at Beatrix, then Alec, then the other survivors with weapons. "Are we willing to distract them long enough for the others to flee? We can't sit back here and let them overwhelm us." Geoff could hear the gunfire behind the lighthouse. The creatures would keep up the pressure until they were overwhelmed or ran out of ammunition.

"Geoff," said Beatrix. "We can't. They'll get slaughtered in those woods."

"They'll get slaughtered here." Geoff turned around. He picked up one of the stakes that Jimmy Bloer had carved. "Half with me. Everyone else, get the kids and old folks out of here."

Everyone nodded and divided. Alec went to protect the kids. Beatrix pumped her shotgun. "I ain't got any family elsewhere. I'll kill those bastards for what they've done."

Geoff nodded and climbed onto the barricade. He felt the blood running down his arm and dripping off the stake. It hurt, but not enough to stop him. He raised Beauty over his head, "We don't have much. We're a town of ghosts and skeletons. When we were left behind we turned on each other. What we've done to ourselves and each other has left this town a carcass. Now these scavengers want to take what's left. I won't have it! Come on!"

The lead creature with the trident hissed. He tapped its trident against the crab monster's leg. The monster chirped and began to move forward slowly, each of its legs moving in sequence.

Geoff leapt from the barricade and charged. *Only have one shot at this.* All he had were the two shells of Beauty and a stake. He had to kill the monster. It only had one weakness that he could see. The dripping, frothing opening of its mouth, a vertical slit of bony mandibles lined with fibers.

He heard the other survivors roar in defiance of this invasion. They vaulted over the barricade. The creatures charged, springing on their crooked legs from the cover of the forest. Geoff didn't pay attention to those. He had his challenge.

The crab monster was easily ten feet wide at the shell. He had to find a way to get to its mouth while avoiding the claws. He ran for the space under its shell. It raised its left claw to crush Geoff into the ground.

He pushed harder. His legs screamed as he fought to gain speed through the sinking mud. The claw came down. He jumped into a roll. The claw struck the ground with earth-shaking force. Geoff stumbled to his feet. The monster's armoured underside almost scraping his scalp. The monster halted. It tried to turn or move back. Geoff kept just under its body, there was no crevice or weak point. Certainly none he could exploit with a stake. He jumped to the side to avoid its legs.

Bingo.

The joint of the leg was, by necessity, unarmoured. Geoff jumped to the side again, bouncing on his toes. He thrust the stake at one of the larger legs but missed. He stabbed it again, driving the point into the soft fibrous muscle. He thrust with the other arm, driving the tip of Beauty's barrel into the joint. He pulled the trigger.

The joint exploded in a burst of shot and blue ichor. The monster screeched. It's weight teetering on its surviving legs. Geoff ran out from under its body, just before the monster fell to the ground. Its whole body quaked and writhed in confusion.

Geoff grinned. *Now to kill it.*

Something hit him in the head. His vision flashed white. He felt his back against the mud. His head rung. He opened his eyes and looked up. A crooked shadow stood over him, lightning flashed, revealing a raised trident.

Geoff's eyes went wide. He rolled to the side. The trident pierced through his jacket, pinning him to the ground. The creature tried to retract the trident, but Geoff locked it with his arm. He reached for Beauty, but the shotgun was gone. The shadow pounced, its wild, yellow eyes and gnashing translucent teeth overwhelming Geoff. He tried to kick the monster away. Its claws raked down his shoulders and chest and left a wicked slice down his face. Blood and pain rolled down his body.

He mustered up his strength and kicked the creature back. Geoff ripped the trident out of the ground. His eyes blurred with rage and blood. He lifted the trident. It felt like a thousand pounds. The creature snarled, trying to get to its feet. Geoff saw its sunken, skeletal torso. Its rubbery slimy skin stretched over thin bones. Claws on its hands and feet like ebony razors. It shrieked.

Geoff roared and drove the trident through its chest. Its body jerked back into the mud. Black ichor poured out of the wound. Geoff slammed it down. Staggering back on weak, sagging legs. Lightning flashed in the sky.

Geoff's weary eyes scanned the battlefield and his heart sank. Townsfolk were tackled and pinned to the ground as their stomachs and faces were torn to pieces. He saw rifles crack from the lighthouse building's roof, bursting open creature's skulls and shattering torsos, but there were more to take their place. Mr. Wan screamed as he blasted a pair of creatures off a fisherman's body, but the man was already dead. Mr. Wan was immediately thrown to the ground by a ravenous creature. Its translucent teeth slammed down into his neck.

Geoff saw Beatrix's strong pale face in the mud. Her eyes wide, staring up at the sky with a vacant gaze. He couldn't make out the outline of her body.

There was a crash. The crab monster had gotten back to its feet, using one claw to counter the loss of the leg. A trail of blue liquid glazed the mud towards the column of escapees. They had tried to head for that exit, but they were moving too slow.

Alec Jonas raised his rifle and fired. The asshole had always been a good shot on a hunt. One of the monster's glowing periscope eyes burst like a tomato. It shuddered in pain, reaching for its face with a claw. It regained its composure and swiped at Alec. He screamed as the bony blades clamped down on his torso. He tried to work the rifle's action, but the monster took its other claw and gripped Alec's throat.

Lightning flashed. All Geoff saw was the silhouette of the monster's sharp jerk. It dropped the wet remains into the mud before pursuing the escapees. Geoff had to stop it.

He got up and ran. He dodged and twisted away from the creatures and the brutal fights in the mud. Chris King and his brothers, James and Tony, fired shotguns into the creatures before one leapt over its falling brethren and tore Chris's throat out. Nicole Jonnason slammed a woodsman axe into a creature's face and managed to decapitate the next, even though her face was raked with claw marks.

Geoff pushed harder, leaping over a creature's final death rattle as one of Brandon Weiber's boys impaled it into the mud.

People screamed as the monster crashed through the birch trees surrounding the trail. Geoff saw Alec's rifle sticking out of the mud. He grabbed it. He felt the life seeping from him. Everything hurt. He worked the rifle's action as he ran.

The screams roared over the storm. Geoff ran as quickly as he could. His boots squishing in and out of the mud. His thighs chafed raw from the rain and blood.

The creature's rear shell dragged across the ground, leaking blue ichor. Geoff escaped the trap of the mud and climbed its rocky armoured back. Hissing echoed behind him. One of the crooked creatures was gliding across the mud in his direction. Its feral eyes lost in bloodlust.

Geoff almost lost his balance as he teetered on the edge of the beast's frontal armour, just behind its eyes. The screeches had almost reached him. Geoff aimed the rifle down into the teeth-lined labia of its mouth.

Just before he pulled the trigger, he felt a body slam into his back. He felt his feet leave the shell. A pair of jaws lined with inch-long teeth pierced his ribs. They crashed in a violent mess of screams, tumbling through the mud and gravel. Geoff's entire body was aflame in a thousand types of pain. He felt his mind retreat from his conscious body to cope. He was watching someone else fight.

The creature who had tackled him lay a few feet from him. Geoff scrambled for the rifle. He gripped the stock just as the creature pounced. He whipped around and caught the creature's jaws on the barrel of the gun.

It screeched in pain. Its throat chortled as it tried to scratch itself free.

Geoff smiled and pulled the trigger.

The back of its head exploded in a spout of black blood. Its entire body sent flying back into a crumpled mess in the mud. Geoff turned to face the crab monster. Its single periscope eye focused on him. Its pair of antennae aimed in his direction buzzing with violent excitement.

Geoff felt the rain pepper his face. Behind him, he heard the fleeing screams of the remaining townsfolk. Geoff had one shot to kill this monster. He couldn't hide beneath it or try to get around it. It was focused on him and only him. There was nowhere to run. If he did, the survivors would die. Geoff worked the action of the rifle. The barrel and mechanism clogged with mud. He prayed to the god who had abandoned them that it wouldn't jam.

The crab monster lumbered towards him on its uneven legs. Geoff charged back; he had one chance. The creature's claws reached out at him. He dove, letting himself slide on the slippery mud. The creature tried to back up, but it couldn't on its damaged leg.

Geoff was right below its face, its gyrating opening of mandibles and slimy fibrous teeth. In its bulbous green eye, Geoff could see his reflection, a dirty little creature covered head to toe in mud and blood. He sprung to his feet and drove the barrel of the rifle into its maw. It screeched, trying to retreat but its weakened legs just tore up the ground.

Geoff pulled the trigger. Silence. It didn't even click. *Jammed.* Geoff was lifted off his feet. Pain shot up around his waist. The monster lifted him above its head with its massive jagged claws. Geoff struggled to escape. He screamed, feeling the pressure building in his ears.

Maybe Olly did get out? Maybe? Hopefully? Geoff honestly doubted it at this point. His mother was dead. His father was dead. His brother was dead. And soon, Geoff would be dead too. *The end of the Karlson line. A two-hundred-year-old family. Dead.*

Maybe that was okay. A family reduced to abuse

and backwards mentality didn't need to be a continued tradition.

Geoff closed his eyes as the other claw reached up for him.

HONK!

A force rocked Geoff's world. He looked down. A huge blue semi slammed into the monster. Its horn trumpeted as it drove the great shelled monster backwards. The monster's claws and legs thrashed. Its rear armour slid across the mud and bodies, turning them up like the blade of a snowplough. Monsters and survivors scattered. The semi drove the monster across the clearing, carving a ditch across the muddy battlefield.

They jerked to a halt at the edge of the cliff. The monster teetered off the edge of the cliff. Its forelegs thrashing, trying to regain its footing. Another push and it would fall headfirst onto the rocks. In its attempt to fight back, it released Geoff. He fell ten feet onto the hood of the semi. Geoff groaned. His lungs gasping and back aching.

He looked into the semi's cab.

Olly sat, huffing, his hair soaked. He gripped the wheel with white knuckles. Their eyes met, and Geoff's pain was replaced with relief.

Olly pressed on the gas, but the massive wheels spun

freely in the sopping mud. The monster had almost regained its footing. It attacked. Geoff rolled off the truck just as a claw crashed down, crumpling the blue hood. Olly kicked open the door and dropped into the mud. Shotgun in hand, he vaulted over one of the monster's legs. Alec's rifle still stuck in its mouth. Olly jammed the rifle barrel down its throat with his boot. Its screeches were choked. He shoved the shotgun into its mouth and pulled the trigger.

The blast was muffled, but the reaction was immediate. The green periscope eye hung limp. Its arms and legs fell with heavy crashes. Olly glanced back at Geoff, through his muddied face was a wide grin and wild, ecstatic eyes.

Geoff saw it before it happened. "Olly! Get back!"

The monster's body slid backwards and vanished. Olly lost his balance and went with it. *NO!* Geoff got to his feet and dove, he gripped blindly, but caught Olly's skinny wrist at the last second. Pain exploded over all of Geoff. Olly dangled off the edge of the cliff with Geoff barely hanging on.

Geoff screamed and pulled. The pressure building in his ears. Olly scrambled onto the edge. They collapsed into the mud. Both of them lay for a second, panting. Rain pattered their faces. Lightning cracked across the blackened sky.

"Good thing you always had the second portion at Thanksgiving, huh?" said Olly.

Geoff couldn't help but burst out laughing. "Thank God that you're the skinny runt."

Olly laughed and got to his feet, he glanced around. "Geoff, we gotta get out of here."

"Where are the others?"

"The mayor got the bus. He was right behind me to pick up the survivors. We gotta go." Olly helped Geoff to his feet.

Geoff groaned and scanned the battlefield. The wind blew hard against his face. Screams echoed through the tempest. There were no survivors left, and the remaining creatures now surrounded the lighthouse.

The lightning flashed more violently than ever. Tendrils of white energy struck the top of the tower. The metal cap for the spotlight exploded in a cascade of sparks. The thunder shook the ground. Energy reverberated off the brick and plaster. The remaining creatures danced around the shower of sparks. In their claws they gripped the severed heads of townsfolk. They swung the heads by the hair and tossed them to each other, like a demented ball game. Another crooked elder creature stood at the center of the orgy of violence. With a trident raised in its finned arms it welcomed the storm.

The lightning and wind bit against the tower. The museum shuddered, metal and wood flying into the distance. Plaster and rubble blew away, leaving a single obsidian obelisk. Glowing yellow and green symbols of an alien language ran up its blackened stone face. The geometric rendition of a serpent climbed its length. The creatures danced in their demented worship, swinging their sacrifices. Lightning struck the obelisk.

"Geoff! We gotta go!" screamed Olly.

"Where?!" They couldn't escape into the park. Geoff was too injured to flee. He pulled up his jeans and realized a huge gash had climbed up his shin. He couldn't even put pressure on it.

Olly threw Geoff's arm over his shoulder. He pointed to the farthest outcropping of the cliff edge. Everyone called it the Dare Spot. Everyone got dared to jump off it. A few even did, until an eight-year-old named Danny Evans died.

"We gotta run," said Olly. "Can you do it?"

Geoff straightened up, despite the blinding pain. "Who got second place at the county track meet?"

"I did."

"There was one other person in your event. I beat thirty others."

"Shut up," said Olly.

They took a breath before sprinting. Geoff closed his

eyes before they got to the edge. His body fell freely. He forced his legs straight. He waited for an eternity to break against the rocks, but he was greeted by the salty cold of the ocean.

He opened his eyes. The ocean was a torrent. Water violently thrashed against them, the current threatening to pull them under. Olly and Geoff swam to a jagged rock covered in algae. Strips of seaweed slapped at them from the thrashing waves. Geoff could barely hang on to the slimy rock. The saltwater washed away the mud, but it also revealed how much he was still bleeding. The salt stung his wounds. Any longer and he feared he would go into shock.

"We'll wade to Pelican Beach!" shouted Olly, pointing south.

"The harbor is closer!" Geoff knew it was more dangerous to go back into town, but he couldn't afford to swim far... He needed to get out of the water.

A pillar of water erupted near them, just below where the lighthouse loomed. A giant scaly body rose out of the water. Its skin was like plates of coral sewn together into a long tube. A serpentine body hovered over the obelisk. Its eel-like face lowered to observe the ritual. A dozen yellow eyes made a line above its huge mouth. A waterfall from its huge jaws lined with sword-sized fangs. Geoff couldn't even guess its size.

The crooked creatures screeched in a chorus. Lightning struck the pillar in a repeated rhythm, as if it followed their demonic song. The unknowable ritual of the crooked creatures was reaching its climax. The storm swirled around the obelisk. An endless hurricane of arcane malice.

"Pelican Beach it is," shouted Geoff, snapping Olly back to attention.

They began their long swim towards safety. Leaving the creatures and the giant serpent, that ancient sea god, to their demonic ritual. The chorus of thunder continued well into the night.

♦

The dark water lapped against the shore. The beach was not made of fine sand, but heavy pebbles and broken shells. The morning sky was solid endless grey. A few nearby trees swayed in the after-storm breeze. The gulls cawed curiously at the pair laying on the shore.

Olly lay on the rough sand, his body jerked awake. He rolled over and coughed up sea water and spittle. He rubbed his eyes, clearing the sand and salt from his face. His vision cleared. A nearby gull cawed.

Geoff lay next to him.

"Geoff?" Olly scrambled to his knees. "Geoff?" He shook his brother. His skin was pale as milk. He was so cold. "Geoff? Geoff? Geoff! Geoff!" Olly continued to shake him, but he got no response. His eyes were shut. Olly pulled up Geoff's sleeve and shirt. His wounds were congealed with blood and sand. They didn't even look infected. He slapped Geoff's face. "Wake up! Wake up, you piece of shit!"

Olly felt the entire world close in around him. He collapsed onto his brother's broad chest. The empty loneliness began to creep into Olly's gut. After everything they'd been through. Geoff had been the strong one. He was the one that got them through hell, whether it was their father or the monsters from the deep. He had been the fighter. The powerful one. The leader.

Olly was alone now.

After what felt like an eternity, Olly got to his feet. The town would meet in the next county over. It would be a half-day walk. Then see what the monsters had left behind, if anything. For all Olly knew, this was the end of the world. Maybe this was just the beginning of the end. He brushed the sand off his ragged clothes.

He surveyed the beach he had visited a thousand times before. He saw a rough stony hill covered in weeds and tall grass.

I have time for now. He owed his brother that muchHe got to work.

He left a pile of stones the crest of that hill. *Geoff would like that.* Someplace high and overlooking the ocean. Almost like he was free from the fate that Dad or the town had given him. Olly continued trudging westward to see if the apocalypse had begun or not. In either case, he would face it alone. But he would face it, nonetheless.

He would miss his brother until the end of his days.

NEOCRUSADERS

The peddler's truck clattered as it rolled down the gravel road. A snake-like trail flanked by rocky, forest-covered slopes on all around. The sky, blinding blue with a few strips of white clouds. The spring air was warm and crisp.

The stranger leaned out the passenger window. Her black hair whipped in the breeze.

The peddler was an older black man with a fuzzy white beard. His purple coat lined with '60s-style tassels. The carriage of his truck was full of odds and ends: a thousand luxury goods, day-to-day essentials, and prized trophies from his decades as this pawn-broker-merchant.

They drove with a cassette in the dash playing some old blues tune.

The truck pulled up to a split in the road. The gravel continued in a curve towards the East, towards the coast.

Where other NeoAnglian cities and towns sat ripe for a peddler's wares.

"Through there, you'll find your way south," said the Peddler, his leathery face unreadable. He pointed up the mountain where the other road led.

The stranger opened the door and dropped out of the truck. She surveyed the grassy valley. The ruined stump of a signpost at the crossroad. Her eyes drifted up the weed-eaten trail leading up towards the mountains only to vanish into the dark forests carpeting the slopes. Her bag and sword hung over her shoulder.

"You sure?"

"Yeah," said the peddler. "If you hurry you can reach the next village by dark. Be careful. Wild folk up there. Ripped Road Creek I think it's called."

She glanced at the trail. "Sounds about right."

"Good luck, stranger," said the peddler as he pulled away. The rickety truck clattered down the road. A trail of dust followed.

When the dust settled, the stranger was completely alone. She adjusted her bag. The silver hilt of her sword glinted in the sunlight. The crossguard with its leaping wolves and tear drop. The weight of the sword and revolver on her hip comforted the stranger. She looked up at the slope. It would be a rough hike trying to reach the other side of the mountain.

The stranger began to walk when a horn blared in the distance. Down the road, a cloud of dust rose. Someone was approaching. The stranger narrowed her eyes. A metallic howl drifted across the valley.

She knew she should probably find cover, but she didn't. Her curiosity overtook her rational interest. Her master would have been sorely disappointed with her. If... however, it was a threat. She would rather get this over with. One way or another. She dropped her bag behind the broken signpost. Her sheathed sword rested on her shoulder.

The trail of dust neared, flanked by huge green mountains. Over the rise she saw five black and white dots approaching. The sputter of their engines grew into a belching roar.

Five men in white tabards with black crosses and shining metal helms rode motorcycles also emblazoned with more black crosses. Censers and rosary chains hung from the handlebars. Weapons and saddlebags hung from the machines' frames.

Each carried a metal lance that glinted in the light. Flags tied to the lances whipped in the wind. White flags with black crosses. The leader wore a red helmet. His chopper hung with chains. A real human skull placed on the front.

The stranger regretted not hiding. *Too late now.* They had certainly seen her. The wind played with her hair as the knights pulled up. Each machine crunched against the gravel. Their engines clicked silent. The red helmed knight threw his leg off his chopper. His compatriots followed.

Each knight wore a Kevlar vest under his tabard. The strips of cloth blowing around their legs along the dusty road. Mail coifs hung around their shoulders, bits of armour strapped to their arms. Swords hung off their belts as did handguns in holsters. They were a walking anachronism. *Everything in this world is.*

They formed a line a dozen yards from the stranger.

After a moment's silence, the leader pulled off his red helm.

His head was wrapped in a hood of greased iron rings. His black hair clung to his forehead, soaked with sweat. His worn face was covered in rough whiskers. Below his sagging grey eyes were tattooed crosses and bible verses.

Silence hung in the air. Wind whistled across the sun-baked road. Trees rustled. A pair of crows watched, fascinated with the proceedings and the promise of corpses. The stranger adjusted her grip on the wire-wound hilt of her sword.

"You the stranger who visited Plygate, Skerhol, and Steigford?" said the knight.

The stranger had visited all those places. All of them had caused problems. From a fight in Plygate on the Franco border, to her wholesale slaughter of a dwarf regiment from Skerhol, to her involvement of the death of the Lord of Steigford. *This ought to be good.*

"Who's asking?"

"Marshal Antioch of the NeoCrusaders."

"What do you want?" said the stranger.

The second crusader. A burly, bear-like warrior with a double-handed axe over his shoulder held up a crumpled piece of paper.

A wanted poster with a bad drawing of the stranger's face. It had her cheeks, chin, and narrow brown eyes, but everything else was wrong. Or was it? She didn't have time for insecurities right now. Two hundred dollars for her head. *That's it?!* It made mention to watch out for a black sword with a wolf-handle.

The stranger's hand fell to her holster.

Two of the junior knights, squires probably, jerked for their handguns. Marshal Antioch hissed. He met the stranger's eyes and nodded. He drew his own revolver, a .44 magnum, and tossed it onto the grass.

The unspoken agreement allowed the stranger to draw her long-barreled .45 and toss it to the side of the road. She undid her cloak, letting the heavy fabric fall to the ground.

Antioch hissed an order. The squires' shoulders sank, but they obeyed along with the rest of the squad. The weapons thunked against the grassy ground. This wasn't going to be a standoff or some duel with firearms. This was a proper fight. Only the better fighter would win. Not the one quick on the draw.

The stranger waited with her scabbard resting across her shoulders.

"You've begun to grow quite the reputation, heathen," said Antioch. Not cruelly, just a statement. "God demands justice. Justice is in God. We are His Blade and His Right Hand. Please come with us."

"Uh, no. Not likely."

"So be it," Antioch put on his helm. His world locked into two narrow slits and suffocating darkness. *At least I don't have to look at that face*, thought the stranger. Antioch drew his sword. A similar longsword to the stranger's, but several inches shorter. He pulled a rosary from his belt. The iron cross hung from a heavy brass chain. The other crusaders did the same.

"'But as for these enemies of mine, who did not want me to reign over them, bring them here and slaughter them before me,'" said Antioch. "So said Luke."

The crusaders began to chain their weapons to their arms. Wrapping the chains tightly around gauntlets and interlacing it around the crossguards of their weapons.

The stranger stared flatly. *Idiots.* Some sort of oath to their weapons and their mission. She had seen it before with princelings and small-time nobles. An oath to never drop your weapon until the mission is over.

Antioch's rough voice whistled through the slits of his helm. "'For he is God's servant for your good. But if you do wrong, be afraid, for he does not bear the sword in vain. For he is the servant of God, an avenger who carries out God's wrath on the wrongdoer.' So said Romans." Metal chains jerked tight. "Amen."

"Amen!" repeated the crusaders.

Disarming them is out of the question. Each man had their weapons chained to one hand. Even the axeman, which made no sense. *Doesn't an axemen have to switch grips? I'm dealing with lunatics... observing some oath more than practicality.*

The stranger drew her sword, gripping the sheath as

a second weapon. *They were heavily armoured...* and the stranger was not. She felt very fragile in her shirt and flannel. Nothing but jeans and boots on her legs.

"Jeru!" barked Antioch. "Salem! Prove yourselves to God and to your brothers."

The two squires roared through their helmets and charged, swords raised.

The stranger burst into a flurry of action. Her black-bladed sword rung off the squires' weapons. Metal cleaved through mail, blood splashed the gravel road. When the dust settled, both faceless fanatics fell to the ground. Blood gushing through their mail coifs and staining their tabards.

Her blade passed in front of her face. A chalky onyx blade splashed with scarlet.

Antioch sighed. "Disappointing. Edessa, Tripoli, with me."

"Don't you assholes have anything better to do?"

"God demands justice."

"Who the fuck made it your duty to hand out God's Justice? You're damn bounty hunters with a gimmick. Let's get this bullshit over with."

The remaining three spread out like predators cornering prey. These were three men well-trained and well-practiced. Two swords and a two-handed axe. The stranger backed up the ragged path with careful steps. Sword and scabbard held defensively.

Her dark eyes drifted from knight to knight. Their faceless helmets, tabards billowing in the wind, the gleam of their weapons. Each step back brought them closer to surrounding her.

Sunlight flashed off Antioch's sword. The stranger winced.

The crusaders charged.

The stranger dashed back. She feinted low and scored a ringing strike on Antioch's helm. *Rung him like a gong. Ha!* He stumbled back as the others attacked.

The stranger dashed back, her head inches from the swinging axe. The other swordsmen followed. The attacks came like a rolling tide of blades. She retreated, climbing up the high ground of the slope.

Then they both came at once. The stranger caught the sword on her own blade, then forced the locked swords to catch the incoming axe at the haft. She grunted, vibrations climbing up her arm. She locked the three weapons together with her sheath.

They began to force her back, her boots sliding in the gravel. A growl echoed from the swordsman's helm. The stranger grit her teeth. She dropped her sheath. In a flash she slammed her knife into the eye slit of the swordsman.

He screamed as blood poured from his visor.

She kicked him over and drove the point of her sword at the axeman. He roared and jumped backwards, a gash bleeding in between the plates on his shoulder.

The stranger gripped her sword with both hands, falling into a low aggressive stance like a cornered lion. She pounced off her toes, driving the point forwards.

"Tripoli!" Antioch rushed into frame, knocking away her blade with his free hand. He smashed a gloved fist into her cheek.

The stranger grunted, forced back. Antioch charged. They were locked in a furious exchange. Blade against blade. Great arcing attacks of longswords, clangs of metal echoing through the valley.

The injured axeman, Tripoli, charged up the slope. Facing two experienced opponents was not a good plan.

The stranger broke from the engagement and sprinted for the cover of the forests. A dark gloomy mess of ivy-covered oaks and elms. The underbrush dripping with fungi and lichen.

Antioch and Tripoli pursued the stranger through the

gloom.

She dashed off the path. Antioch followed, dashing around a huge oak with his sword raised. The stranger vanished. Tripoli stood a few meters down the path, blood running down his arm.

Locked within their helmets, the NeoCrusaders were vulnerable in the claustrophobic gloom of the forest.

A twig snapped.

Antioch whipped around, but it was too late. The stranger burst from the undergrowth and slammed sideways into Tripoli.

The sword pierced through the side of his vest and out the other side. He roared, unable to swing his axe with the way it was chained to his arm.

The stranger wrenched the sword from the knight. Blood pouring onto the ground. She spun, swinging her blade in a hard, horizontal arc. The blade bit into his neck, just below the helm, it crunched through the mail and the flesh of his throat.

Blood spurted down the crusader's front. Scarlet covering the black and white tabard.

Tripoli fell to his knees, already dead, his head lolled back on a few surviving tendons and the remains of the mail coif. The body collapsed, blood pooling high enough to cover up the crucifix.

The stranger flicked the blood off her sword.

"You'll regret that, woman," said Antioch through his dented helm. "God demands blood for blood."

"What fucking Sunday school did you go to? Did you have a touchy-feely priest or did the prohibition on masturbation short-circuit your brain?!" She resumed a defensive stance, now downhill at a disadvantage.

Antioch charged, two-handing his sword.

The stranger took the brunt of his attack. She tried to flow around him, but he attacked with a barrage of overhand strikes. She parried the attacks. Metal rang through the wet forest gloom. Birds scattered with each vicious strike.

Blades locked. "God wills it!" screamed Antioch.

The stranger slid her blade down Antioch's, trying to weave around his guard. The edge crashed into his crossguard, snapping the copper chains. He side-stepped and scored a cut on her arm. She grunted. Blood ran down her elbow. He backhanded her across the face. The stranger stumbled back, the metallic taste of blood filling her mouth.

"God wills it!" roared Antioch, raising his sword.

The stranger blocked, both blades bit into each other.

The mysterious black metal holding up better than the steel. Antioch growled, his rage-fueled strength overwhelming the stranger's desperation.

He pressed his dented helm close to her face. "God wills you die."

The broken chains jingled off his wrist.

The stranger spat a spray of blood against the visor. Antioch jerked back. The stranger grabbed the rosary chain and yanked the crusader's arm. Gaining control of his weapon.

She drove her blade up into his armpit and out the side of his neck, the blade poking up beneath the mail coif. Blood seeped down the tabard. His sword slipped from his fingers. His gloved hand pawed at her throat with the final vestiges of his strength. His voice wheezed as his lungs deflated

The stranger grimaced and kicked him over. The body crumpled to the forest floor.

The stranger stood in the gloomy trail, chest heaving, sweat streaming down her face and painting for air. Pain vibrated across her face and bleeding arm. The adrenaline left her shaking, but she still had a long hike ahead.

She glanced at the gruesome gash on her arm. "These assholes are going to get annoying."

The stranger returned for her bag. She sealed her gash with the remains of her superglue and wrapped it with a piece of the crusader's white tabard.

"Pieces of fucking fanatical shit..." she grunted, pulling the fabric tight. She had barely spent four months traveling from Franco through NeoAnglia. Now she already had bounty hunters trailing after her.

She raided their pockets for ammunition, money, and whatever else she could find that was useful. She took their rosaries and any of precious objects to sell. She strapped on their kneepads and spaulders and continued her journey, more prepared than she had been.

The Wrong Side of the Veil demanded it.

SACRIFICE

The van crunched against the gravel road. Chris looked out the window to the pine trees passing by in a blur. His round, flat face and brown eyes watched the light glint off the mountains.

The vehicle reeked of cigarette smoke. They followed the winding, narrow road through the Rocky Mountain interior. Lucas and Curt argued back and forth over... something... Chris wasn't paying attention. They had left Radium two hours ago, heading south towards the festival.

Stanley, the tall triathlete, was reading a book. His University of Calgary shirt stretched across his chest. Chris had been quiet since they entered the Rockies. He still wore a long-sleeved shirt, even with the hot summer heat.

They eventually found the right route, a few miles from a tiny valley town called Brenton. In a large public park rose a sea of tents, slightly larger than the town. Mountains towered in every direction. A stage was set up near the edge of a small lake. A caution rope warned people to stay away from the water and respect the environment.

Zero chance of that, thought Chris.

The four friends unloaded and carried their tents and coolers. Curt found a spot beneath a tree, the ground covered in needles. The sweet smell of pine held back the usual smells of a festival camp. The weed, the vomit, the garbage.

Curt laughed as he pitched his tent. "This is gonna be wicked. Deathsteel starts at six, More Pain at seven." He listed off the bands playing over the next two days with childish fixation.

Chris had stopped listening to a lot of the new underground bands over a year ago. He had a few he liked. He was only really excited to see the headliner, The Pretty Reckless. He missed all the other times they toured back home.

"Need help?" asked Stanley, picking up Chris's tent bag.

Chris nodded. Stanley was tall, white, and painfully good looking, with short brown hair. In comparison, Chris felt small and with messy black hair, painfully aware he was probably one of the only Asian kids at the festival. His friends were cool. He had known them all for a long time. The festival just felt overwhelming after everything.

Curt already had a beer opened. Calling to a tent across a clearing where a bunch of girls were preparing themselves for the part. They laughed, calmly flipping him off. They were painting a banner for one of the bands.

With their tent set up, Chris and Stanley sat in lawn chairs. Stanley handed Chris a beer. "You all right?" he asked.

"Fine," said Chris.

"You sure?"

"I'm fine, really."

"Okay," said Stanley. "Just keep me posted if you need anything. If you—"

"I said I'm okay. Jesus, man. I'm not a kid." Chris caught himself. "Sorry."

"It's all right." Stanley paused. "We're both too sober." He pulled out the Jack Daniels.

The sun began to set as the park filled with more and more tents. Curt and Lucas came back from visiting friends at the other end of camp. Chris and Stanley were both buzzed, discussing negative and positive conceptions of freedom.

"He boring you yet, Chris?" joked Lucas. They all laughed.

Stanley leapt to his feet. *"We few, we happy few, we band of brothers; For he to-day that sheds his blood with me—"*

Lucas made a farting noise. Stanley flipped him off.

"Nah, man," said Chris. "Need to expand your mind—"

They blew raspberries at Chris and Stanley. They all laughed, passing more drinks.

"What took you guys so long?" said Chris. "I thought you were just visiting Tracy?"

Lucas laughed. "Someone—" (meaning Curt), "—had to meet her new roommate."

"Did someone finally swap V-cards?" said Stanley.

"Fuck you, man," barked Curt. "I knew what the clitoris was before you even knew it existed."

"It exists?"

"Dude," said Chris. "You're just not trying hard enough. Remember, come hither motions."

They all laughed. Lucas glanced at his phone in his hand. They had all agreed to leave them at home, but Lucas protested. They eventually agreed an emergency phone was probably a good idea. He was really just waiting for his girlfriend to text him.

Chris slowly came out of his shell. "The real question. Tell me when…" He held his hands to his chest, cupping invisible breasts. He slowly started making them bigger. They laughed louder.

They laughed and shared stories. Many of them inappropriate. It felt good for Chris. Something they hadn't had in a very long time. *Maybe this wasn't a bad idea.* The sun finally began creeping behind a mountain. Covering the whole valley in shadow. Lights sprang up on the stage, music began to play from the speakers. The openers would play in about thirty-five minutes.

The crowds began to near the stage. Goths with chains hanging from their noses. Girls with dyed hair and Led Zeppelin shirts. Old-style metalheads with long hair hanging around their faces. Punks with shaved heads and combat boots. A few gangs of freaks with masks, banners, and costumes. The really crazy ones.

As the group neared the crowd, Curt ran up to one girl in a tiki mask. She wasn't wearing a shirt, only paint and gemstones. Stanley raised an eyebrow when he saw money and a plastic bag transfer hands.

Whatever, thought Chris; it was his own life. Chris saw

Stanley frown disapprovingly.

Chris reeked with his long sleeves. Through the drunken haze, they moved into the thick crowd of people. The mist of weed, sweat, and hormones hung above their heads. A claustrophobic horde of cackling, screaming people.

When the first band came out, that's when all hell broke loose.

Hundreds of people jumping and dancing. A thousand voices screaming along. A sea of heads rippling to the rhythm. Birds flew from the trees to escape the noise. Yeah, it was pretty mono-cultural, but Chris had always preferred this kind of music.

Chris closed his eyes. Letting the music flow over him. Feeling the expert guitar work, the heavy pounding of the drums, the shrieking lyrics. It washed over him with lurid artistry. He felt freedom for the first time in a long time, like he was finally able to step out of his own body.

Stanley swayed along next to him.

Good, he's having fun too. Chris didn't know how guilty he felt. *Maybe a lot.* Stanley only came for Chris's sake. To keep him out of trouble. To keep him safe. Chris knew his parents had basically begged Stanley to join this trip.

Curt popped up. "Come on!" Urging them on to come deeper into the crowd. Lucas was farther up, jumping around with their other friends. A few others they knew from work and old high school friends. Chris and Stanley didn't know them that well. Lucas would stop constantly, just to check his phone.

"We're fine here. Thanks, bud," said Stanley.

"You two are such pussies, come on. I've been planning this for months!"

"We're fine," said Stanley, more firmly. "Thanks. Just go have fun."

"Not without you two!" Curt tried to use his bulk to push them farther, arms wrapped around them. Chris clenched his teeth. Curt pushed too hard. Stanley saw the pain on Chris's face.

Stanley shoved off Curt. "Stop being an asshole. We'll join you in a bit."

Curt frowned. "Fine." He realized he had gone too far and rejoined the others without a word or apology.

"We should join them." Chris rubbed his wrist.

"Do you actually want to?"

Chris shrugged.

"They'll be fine. I didn't come here for them."

Chris nodded. Staring at the stage. Watching the spikey-haired singer wiggle her tongue. The music boomed. The pair had been friends since childhood. No one knew Chris as well as Stanley did. He was the only one who didn't pepper him with questions about the hospital.

A lot of secrets had come out over the last year. A lot of stuff had happened since they all graduated high school. A lot of things he felt guilty about hiding. Guilt which only added to the anxiety that blanketed his every thought. He wanted to be here. He wanted to see his friends have fun. He just didn't know if he needed to be here for that. Was he bringing everyone down? He never wanted them to come to the hospital. *They all did, though. Even Curt.*

"Want to head back?" asked Stanley.

"Hell no. Come on. Let's go dance with the fat man."

They pushed closed to the stage. Curt was jumping around, spinning like an overweight child. Lucas's red hair bounced with his every movement, he grinned when Chris and Stanley pushed into their circle. He tried to get them to jump around with him, but quickly stopped. Realizing immediately what Curt had to be reminded of.

Lucas glanced at his phone again, being jostled by other metal heads.

That new girl is going to destroy him. A little brunette

with an attitude, but mostly she was just insecure. Christy? Chloe? Chris couldn't remember. Anyway, she took her issues out on Lucas. Bullied him really. Controlled him. Apparently, this trip had been a big controversy.

Chris let the music wash over him again. The rolling guitar work. The haze of steam and screams held the crowd in its flux of penned-in chaos. Curt spun around, head thrown up in the air. He bumped into people. Some laughed, some joined in, but some glared.

Chris looked out over the lake. He thought he saw fireflies. Little dots of light hovering, making the lake glitter. Then he saw two more lights. A pair of them. Equally spaced apart, like eyes. Pale coloured, like a cat's eyes in low light. *What is that?*

Stanley elbowed him. "What's up?"

Chris shook his head before looking back, but nothing was there. "Nothing." He turned back.

Stanley wasn't watching.

"Look out!"

Curt, deliberately unaware of his surroundings, slammed into Stanley full force. Stanley's feet left the ground. He knocked Chris into circle of combat-booted punks. The wind knocked out of him.

One punk, short with a blonde buzz cut, swore, "Get off me, fucking piece of—CHINK!" He kicked Chris in the back. Chris tried to roll away but took another sharp kick to the back of the head. Pain spread through the back of his head.

In an instant, Curt had the punk by the collar raised off the ground. The pale little shit looked terrified in the fat man's grip.

"What did you fucking say?!" Roared Curt. "You want to say it again?"

Stanley got Chris to his feet. His lungs burned. He struggled to suck oxygen. The other punks turned, lethal drunken hate in their eyes. Chris shrunk behind Stanley, finally catching his breath. *No no no no. Not this. Why did they have to do this...?*

Lucas saw how bad the situation could be in mere instants. Seconds would turn this into a riot. Security hadn't noticed them. Not yet anyways.

I have to say something. Do something.

"Just put him down, Curt," yelled Chris, rubbing his head. "It ain't worth it!"

Curt turned, his face bright red. He shoved the skinhead back into his friends. They all looked ready to charge. Their wild eyes fueled on God-knows-what. Not a sober brain to be seen.

Chris rubbed the back of his head. "Come on." They all nodded and walked away. One skinhead flipped them off. The short one raised a fist. "Hey, white power!"

Stanley looked disgusted, but he didn't launch himself at them. Chris grabbed his shoulder. "Come on, let's just go back to the tent."

Stanley nodded.

Curt looked hurt. "Where you guys going! Stick Meat is next!"

"We'll be back," said Stanley, lying through his teeth. "Don't stop." The pair vanished into the horde of people.

♦

Back at the tent, they popped open more beers.

"Fucking assholes."

"Yeah," agreed Chris.

"Curt needs to fucking grow up…"

Chris looked at his feet. "Oh."

"What?"

"You blame Curt for that?"

"I blame him for acting like a teenager."

Chris frowned. "He's just having fun…"

Stanley shrugged. They were both forgetting that the shithead skinheads were the real problem. Chris knew Curt wasn't a bad guy, but his immaturity wasn't anything new. He'd been frustrated with Curt for a long time. They all had. It had been building. Stanley was just more open about it.

First, it was the smoking, something none of them had ever done. Something Curt had never done. That is, until he met Liza. Then it was the drinking. Which wasn't on its own bad. It was the quantity. Drinking until he puked, once all over Stanley's parents' couch, and breaking things as a big joke. Then it was dusk-to-dawn partying every other night. Even before exams.

Then Liza cheated on him.

Instead of stopping the worst of his behavior, Curt doubled down. He hadn't stopped partying since graduating a year ago. Which wasn't bad, plenty of people did that. It was his more toxic tendency to spill his problems into other people's lives. He just wallowed in his own misery. Living in a rat-infested apartment and thinking it was fine, then getting offended when no one wanted to stay at his place.

Curt wasn't bad, the things he was doing weren't bad on their own. It was the extreme he took it. Everything to the absolute worst level.

Chris had stopped replying to any of Curt's messages. Barely any contact until Chris was in the hospital. Stanley maintained a similar distance and expressed the same feelings. He avoided the group even longer than Chris had.

The music rumbled in the distance. The pyrotechnics from the show lit up the cloud cover. *When had clouds come in?* Chris sniffed. "I didn't know it was supposed to rain."

"It wasn't."

They sipped their beers.

"When did it get so complicated?" said Stanley.

Chris frowned. "Your life isn't so complicated."

Stanley looked at his feet. He knew what it meant. He was the only one in the group who hadn't moved out. He and Chris were the only ones who were going to university. They knew what their future looked like, or had at least delayed the need to choose. Stanley was the one who lived the easy life. No rent, no issues, no stress.

Stanley nodded, ashamed about his luck. "True, but life *is*."

Chris nodded. He could agree with that. He pushed it all from his mind. Letting the warmth of the alcohol take over him. He passed out in the lawn chair. The music echoed over the mountains.

♦

Chris woke up to rain pattering against the tent. It was painfully cold. His head pounded. He groaned sitting up in his sleeping bag. He checked his watch; it was almost one. Stanley's bag was empty. Chris didn't remember getting himself to bed.

He rubbed his eyes with the heels of his hands. He pulled on a fresh shirt.

With a groan and a crawl, he unzipped the tent. He almost burst out laughing.

Stanley and Curt were both passed out. Just under the branches so they didn't get dripped on too much. Curt was curled up in a ball in a nook of the tree. A sweater draped over his shoulders. Stanley was still in his lawn chair. His legs were soaked from the rain. He snored with his head hanging back.

The smell of campfires permeated the grey morning. The tents formed narrow alleys. A maze of domed and peaked nylon stretched in all directions. Everything piled on each other as if to say, "Sorry, let me sneak by."

The forecast said sunny all weekend. Everyone was waking up from their hangovers. The occasional heave or groan would echo nearby. People laughed. A girl or guy with messy hair and disheveled clothing would pass by.

Lucas unzipped his tent. "Morning, loser. You missed a great time last night."

Chris knew he meant it as a joke.

He forced himself to not go back into his sleeping bag. *Can't they just let me disappear?* He'd come back when he was ready. When he felt he needed to come back.

Lucas instantly knew he made the wrong joke. He changed the subject. "You hungry?"

"Sure."

Lucas reached from his tent, not wanting to get into the rain and pulled the cooler closer to him.

Chris saw something in the corner of his vision. A small shadow ran behind the tree. He stared. Trying to see what it was. *Maybe a bird?*

"What the fuck!" yelled Lucas. Stanley jolted awake. "What! What!" He fell out of his chair.

Lucas groaned. "All the fucking food has gone moldy." He held up the bagels they brought. The golden brown rings were covered in green and white fluff. He dug. He pulled out the bags of fruit and veggies, also covered in mold. He opened an energy bar. It fell apart like wet sand. "What the hell! Everything's gone bad. We just bought this yesterday!" He pulled out the beef jerky. It looked like curdled beef stew.

Stanley's eyes went wide. He scrambled to behind the tree. Retching violently.

Curt woke up, sniffing the smell of vomit.

"You see this shit?!" said Lucas. "We got ripped off by fucking Walmart."

Stanley stumbled back around, looking green. He avoided looking in the cooler.

They checked the other cooler. The one with the booze. *How can booze go bad?* Stanley opened the one bottle of wine they brought. He sniffed the Merlot. "Vinegar? It's never been opened."

"What the hell is going on?" asked Chris.

"We got ripped off," barked Lucas.

Stanley sniffed a bottle of water before sipping it, "We got ripped off from a ma-n-pa bakery, Walmart, *and* the liquor store? No freaking way."

Lucas shrugged. He pulled out his phone. "I am not getting much service. I think I saw something in town."

"What the fuck!" shrieked a female voice.

One of the girl's across from them was looking in her

THE VEILED SAGAS: BLOODIED

own cooler, then into a bag of food. One of her friends was hugging a bucket. Another one looked as distressed as she fiddled with her phone.

Lucas called, "You guys too?" The girl looked up. "Everything gone bad?"

"You too?"

"Yeah, everything. Even the beef jerky."

Lucas and the girl shouted back and forth the same confused conversation the rest of them just had. She was pretty. Dark hair, nose ring, with big blue eyes. Reminded Chris of one of the girls he had a crush on in high school. *What was her name?*

Then he looked past her.

Behind her, between another pair of tents was a small hunched figure. It was reaching into another cooler. Rummaging around. It couldn't have been a foot tall. A thin, almost-emaciated body with splotchy pimples across its back. Its fist-sized head had a large pair of ears, the cartilage torn. It wore nothing but a dirty cloth vest and pants made from skins.

Chris blinked. Trying to focus.

It was gone.

What the fuck?

Curt came running from checking in on their other friends. He stumbled, still a little drunk from the night. He huffed, collapsing under the shelter of the tree. "Same thing over there. A lot of people's food got wrecked."

They all looked at each other. It couldn't be a coincidence. They couldn't all have just bought bad food.

"Maybe someone sabotaged it?" said Lucas.

"Someone would have noticed if it happened to this many people," said Stanley.

Chris drank some water. "Security is looking into it anyways…"

Lucas put down his phone. *Finally ignoring that girl?* Thought Chris. "Maybe it's the climate?"

"You ever seen beef jerky congeal from being in the mountains?" said Stanley.

"Rain?"

They were desperate for answers.

The rain had died down.

"What should we do?" asked Chris. *Stanley always had a backup plan. Or Curt will know someone.*

"Should be a store in town," said Lucas.

Curt grinned. "Yeah. We'll get some hoagies and chips!

Some fresh stuff!"

"Yeah, and a hundred other hungry metalheads. Prices will skyrocket," said Stanley. "I thought there were vendors?"

Curt shook his head. "Checked. Sold out, whatever extra they had left got hit the same. Rotten burgers look surprisingly like Bonnie Shatski's cooch."

"Maybe it's the plague or something? Some kind of infection that sweeps through?" said Lucas.

"Sweeps through plastic bags and sealed containers?" said Stanley.

Lucas flipped him off. "Hey, just 'cause you're right doesn't mean you haf'ta be a cunt about it."

Stanley pulled his rain jacket tighter. He had brought two. One for Chris. *Over-prepared bastard.* Chris was thankful for it, though.

Curt wiped his face. "Chris, want to come with me on a food run? See what we can find?"

"S… Sure."

"I'll come too…" said Stanley.

"Nah," said Curt. "We got it. You guys sit tight."

"But…" said Stanley. Chris gave him a nod. Stanley

shut his mouth. *I can handle being alone with Curt. He's an old friend. No bullshit.* Chris followed Curt.

They headed to town.

♦

The local grocery store was total anarchy. Metalheads, hipsters, and groupies of every stripe were trying to find food. Chris saw the skinheads smoking at the edge of the crowded parking lot. The poor supervisor and two local girls couldn't scan and charge fast enough before more hungry, hungover, and frustrated concert goers put more items in front of them.

Chris followed Curt. It didn't take them long before they discovered that huge swaths of the inventory were rotten. A fourteen-year-old shovelled the mess into a bin. The sour smell was overpowering. Chris picked up a pear, turning it over. It had a huge rotten bite mark in it.

He heard a conversation while Curt moved on ahead.

"I just came in this morning and everything was like this..." said a thin man wearing an apron. *Maybe the owner?* His lip frowned with a tiny pencil moustache.

"The whole fridge was the same this morning," said an older gentleman with his wife. "A big stinking mess. I thought maybe it had broke and I just didn't notice, but the slime was cold. The bloody thing still hummed away. The

Kraus's were the same."

"A fucking disaster," said the owner.

"Language," said the wife.

"Sorry Marg… Just lost a ton of business. Stocked up extra for the concert. I'll be cleared out before the end of the weekend."

"With nothing for your own neighbors?"

"Buy what you can, Al. I got a business to run."

"Not on this pension I can't," hissed the husband.

Chris watched them leave. The owner entered the backroom. As the door swung, Chris noticed something on the wall, around knee-level. Three long claw marks buried deep into the plaster.

"Hey!" barked Curt. "No one's gone for the beans yet! Score!"

Chris turned back, but he couldn't see the scratches. The wall looked perfect.

♦

On the way back, the trees and mountains flew by in a blur. With fresh bags of food, Curt chirped incessantly about the one time in the hot tub with Bonnie Shatski. After all the gory details were retold, Curt paused.

A long pause.

Finally.

Curt sighed.

Shit.

"You missed that party too, huh…"

Chris remembered. He had been studying. *Had to make Dad proud.* He hadn't bothered to check his phone. He might have heard it ring, but he ignored it. He was trapped in his claustrophobic residence room trying to pound data into his skull. By the time he saw the messages it was too late and ignored it further.

He focused on the mountains. Hoping the moment would pass.

Curt continued. "I guess you had other things to do."

"I'm sorry…" said Chris.

"No. No! I get it," said Curt. "It just makes me sad, you know, like you don't want to hang out with us."

Chris gripped the armrest. His heart pounded. *Breathe. We're almost there.* He watched the dense pine trees go by in a blur. A mountain lake like a disk of blue glass sat in the valley. He breathed. Praying the silence would drop the subject.

But Curt didn't work that way. "You've just missed so much. I feel bad. You've missed so many great times."

Chris watched the curb go by. *How dangerous would it be to jump out?* Surely, he wouldn't die. He'd done painful things to get out of these interactions before. He just needed to do it. He tried to breathe, but his lungs wouldn't listen. His pulse pounded in his ears.

Curt slowed as he curved the road.

"Why didn't you come out with us?"

Chris squeezed the door handle. He readied himself. He needed to escape this. He was trapped. His breathing and pulse elevated. He was caught between the two boulders of school and friends. *You're smart, you can skip,* Curt had said a dozen times. *Come hang out with us. What's more important?*

He grabbed the door handle. He...

CRASH!

The vehicle jerked. Curt swerved, trying to stay on the narrow road. Brakes squealed. A car behind them honked. It was the skinheads. They pulled ahead, flipping Chris and Curt off and screaming obscenities.

The pair got out.

A deer lay dying by the road.

"Fuck…" said Curt.

Chris stared at the deer. It whimpered. Both its antlers were broken off. Its entire side was a red mess. Long strips of torn tissue and bloodied skin. Its back leg was broken. Bone splitting through the fur.

He knew what blood looked like.

He remembered how a blade touched skin.

"Chris!" barked Curt. "Come on. There's nothing we can do."

Chris nodded. When he looked back, the deer had stopped moving. He turned back to the vehicle. The headlight was broken, but he didn't see any blood. It was clean. *Wouldn't the car be covered in blood if the deer had been cut by the bumper?*

They drove back in silence.

♦

Back at the camp, they got a small fire going to warm the cans. "Thank God. I still haven't gotten any reception. No one has…" said Lucas. "Chloe is gonna worry."

"Oh, that ball and chain," laughed Curt. "Haha, she's gonna break your heart."

He said it like a joke, which was why Lucas laughed.

Stanley nodded. "Thanks."

They opened the cans and got ready to eat. Stanley raised a spoon to his lips. Chris looked down. It wasn't beans. It was a can of dead, putrid, white worms.

Stanley opened his mouth.

Chris leapt from his chair. "Don't!" He slapped the spoon away from his mouth. Pale worms spilled on the grass.

Everyone jumped. Swearing. Curt howled with laughter, pouring his can of worms into the fire.

Stanley's brown eyes immediately went to Curt. He grabbed the big man by the collar, "What the fuck! You think this is some kind of fucking joke?"

Curt shoved him off. They were both big. Curt was fatter, Stanley was leaner. A varsity swimmer. "Fuck you, man. You think I did this? I'm starving too."

Stanley glared.

"Don't look at me like that. I didn't plan any of this shit! I just wanted a weekend with my friends!"

Thunder rumbled over the mountain. The grey sky was darkening to the west. The rain was coming back, harder and darker.

"This weekend is down the tubes, man…" said Stanley.

"We need to pack up and head home."

Chris knew Stanley was right. It sucked, but he was right. This concert wasn't worth it.

Curt paled. "What? No! We have to stay! We spent too much money, drove too far. I spent so much time planning."

Lucas looked terrified. The prospect of going home. He clutched his phone with white knuckles.

Stanley crossed his arms. "We're going to pack up and head home. Before it gets any worse. There might be food in Radium or someplace."

Curt shoved his fat finger into Stanley's face. "Some of us can't afford to give up this easily. We have to stay. *We* spent too much on the tickets!"

Stanley glared. "What do you mean?"

"Nothing."

"Say it."

Curt's face was beet red again. "Not all of us have the spare change to throw around. Not all of us have Daddy's money. The rest of us pay rent."

Stanley didn't move.

Curt wasn't an angry person; he laughed off *everything.* Something darker slipped out. Not his everlasting partying.

"You're such an arrogant bastard. Thinking you're better than us. Too good to come hang out. Always having better things to do. What's more important than your friends?!"

"I don't know, maybe life goals? Being a responsible human being."

Curt spat on the ground. "You're not! Don't even pretend you are! You're just a daddy's boy with all the money in the world. Free to go to school, no rent. Then you drop everyone like *you're* the one with problems. Fuck you!"

Stanley stepped forward, pressing into Curt. "And you're just an overgrown manchild. So deep in debt you can't see how much you've fucked up your own life. I *am* lucky I can still be at home, but I don't fucking waste it. So, don't act like I am fucking around. You had plenty of chances. Remember that scholarship that you dropped 'cause there was *too much paperwork*? You're an idiot." Stanley got right in Curt's face. Rain soaked both of them. "We're heading home."

Chris watched silently.

Lucas stepped out from the shelter of the tree. "Come on, guys. We're supposed to be friends."

Stanley turned back, tossing empty bottles and garbage into a bag. "We haven't been friends for a long time. Let's stop kidding ourselves. Let's pack up and get the fuck out of here."

"No," said Lucas. "We can't. Not yet. I… Not yet."

"Oh my God, man! You really that scared of her?"

Lucas grimaced.

"You've been texting her all weekend!"

"No, I haven't!" barked Lucas, finding his center. "I haven't had reception all day! I… I was just waiting to see if she sent me anything… If I didn't reply quickly—"

"If you're really that terrified of her, then you *shouldn't* be with her!"

Chris agreed, even though he never felt it was his place to say. Curt rubbed his forehead. "She's an awful bitch. We all know it. Except you."

"Hey, fuck you man!" said Lucas. "Who are you to talk!?"

"He's right," said Stanley. "All she ever does is bully you. Then the off time we're all out, you're always on the phone with her. She's got you wrapped around her finger."

Lucas looked down unsure of what to say.

They all paused. The rain pattered. A few people passed by. Arms carrying rolled up tents and wet belongings.

The camp had steadily been shrinking. Streams of people leaving, giving up on the weekend. It was only a portion of the campsite, but it was brutal to the morale of the festival. Chris agreed, he didn't even want to come. He just needed Curt to stop whining.

"Give me the keys," said Stanley.

Curt froze.

"No."

Stanley held out his hand. "Come on, man. Don't be such a baby."

"We're not going anywhere. Just give it a chance."

"Give me the fucking keys!" Stanley stepped forward.

"No."

Lucas shuffled. "Come on, Curt. Give him the keys. We'll go to a bar on the way home. Find a motel and have a party. It'll be a blast."

Curt looked down.

That's when they all looked at Chris. *No. No. No. Don't ask me.* His heart started pounding. He looked for a way out. He knew there wasn't. He couldn't look away. He took a breath. He didn't even want to come…

"Let's… just go home."

Stanley nodded. Curt dropped the keys on the ground. They all knew it was Chris that had the deciding vote. After everything he'd been through, they'd been skirting around him or making exceptions for him. He hated it.

But right now, we need to leave.

Before long they had packed everything and loaded it into the van. Stanley got into the driver's seat. Other groups were almost ready to leave. Some poor volunteers in yellow vests stood freezing in the rain. The valley was locked away in miserable darkness.

The rain hammered the windshield. It was getting dark. Chris sat in the passenger seat. Curt sat in the back, defeated.

Stanley turned the key.

Nothing.

He turned it again.

Nothing.

"What the hell?" he turned it again.

Chris leaned forward. "What's wrong?"

"I don't fucking know." He turned the key. Nothing happened. Stanley whipped around to look at Curt.

"Don't look at me," said Curt. "I already got to pay for

the dent from that deer."

"I'll pay for it," said Stanley as he got out. "If you're so sore about it."

Stanley got out and opened the hood. Rain running down their jackets. Chris sat, watching the trees. Other groups seemed to be having car trouble too. He saw a shadow dance between the vehicles. He rubbed his eyes. *Need to get them checked.* Too many weird things that weren't there.

He saw Curt in the rearview mirror. The big man looked so defeated.

Chris knew what that was like. Feeling the whole world overwhelming you while simultaneously leaving you behind. Feeling like you're failing everyone no matter how hard you try. He adjusted his sleeves. He sighed. "It'll be okay. We'll have plenty of fun on the way back."

"It's just not the same."

Chris shrugged.

"You guys will just go back to school and ignore me. Like nothing matters."

Chris was silent.

"Why does everyone abandon me?"

Curt opened his mouth again, ready to whine. Chris

cut him off. "Oh, will you just shut the fuck up? You're so fucking toxic and far up your own ass. You want to know why me and Stan stopped joining you? Cause we have stuff to do besides partying. We have shit to do! And you guilt us for having them!"

Curt looked at Chris. Lucas was looking too. Chris was shaking. His head felt light. He never thought he could do that. Actually standing up to someone. Saying what he was really thinking. He felt proud of himself. For a moment. *Maybe things would get better, and they could all move on.*

"Some friend you are," hissed Curt.

"A friend would understand." Chris kicked open the door. "To have friends, you got to be a friend." Rain hit his face. He asked Stanley how they were doing.

"Not good. Spark plug is gone," grunted Stanley.

"You guys too?" said a passing volunteer.

Turned out a lot of people got hit. Almost three dozen vehicles. Security had already called a local auto shop. Police and park rangers were notified and on their way. Too many things had gone wrong. It was dark out and freezing cold. There was a rumble. The festival concert continued, despite the setbacks. Stanley frowned.

Chris knew how much he had wanted to see the show. The Pretty Reckless would be on soon. He saw the pathetic look on Curt's face.

"Do we want to go check it out?" said Chris. "We can watch for a bit. Then head out? We're all loaded up anyways."

Stanley thought about it. He looked over his shoulder at the streaming crowds. He took a moment before nodding.

Curt's face glowed when they said they would watch the show for an hour. The rain paused. The clouds broke up over the valley. Moonlight dancing amongst the crowd.

They rejoined the crowd of bouncing heads. Chris smiled, bobbing along to the music. Stanley loosened up. Letting himself rock around to the rolling guitar riffs. *He could have fun.* Chris let himself jump around. Lucas had put away his phone. He was present. Not lost in arguments that he felt were coming. His mess of red hair bobbing with the crowd. Curt was jumping, but not out of control. *He could have fun without being a douche about it... when he wanted to.* Maybe he just needed to be reminded of that.

Caught up in his thoughts, Chris didn't see the line of crooked figures advancing through the forests. No one noticed. The pounding music and howling crowd was the perfect collection of distracted victims. The horned predators advanced unseen.

Then the real show began. Over the sound system a

voice cried, "Welcome! The Pretty Reckless!"

Taylor Momsen, Cindy Lou Who in the flesh, stepped out with her band. Grown up into a satanic rock goddess. Her ragged platinum blonde hair hung around her bare shoulders. The crowd screamed in unison. She raised her hands. Her torn shirt read, "I Fuck for Satan." Black electrical tape was visible under her shirt, covering her nipples. The screams grew louder.

Chris smiled.

Maybe things were going to get better?

She opened her mouth for the first note.

The screams grew more erratic.

Then she cocked her head and said into the mic. "What the fuck!"

A jagged spear flew through the air and impaled the rock star through the stomach. Planting her to the drum set. Blood sprayed the front row. Horrified screams erupted in every direction.

Chris turned.

Now he knew why people were screaming.

A line of dark figures charged into the crowd from the forest line. Metalheads and punks screamed, fleeing for their lives. Metal glinted. People fell to the ground. Chris couldn't see the dark figures, but he saw the swinging metal weapons, arcs of scarlet in the air, and horns. Long curved horns.

Security reacted the only way they knew how. They charged the commotion. Completely convinced it was some shitheads in masks. Then blood splattered their uniforms and more bodies fell to the ground.

They broke. They ran. Everyone did. The crowd devolved into pure chaos.

Stanley grabbed Chris by the shoulder. "Come on!" They ran.

The screaming almost blew Chris's eardrums out. That wasn't even the worst part. It was the sound the horned attackers made. A deep choked bleating. Halfway between man's yell and the scream of a goat being slaughtered.

People crashed into each other to escape through the campsite and towards the vehicles, the only escape route they knew. Stanley held on to Chris, who tried to keep close to the others. They were forced to follow the crowd into the campsite.

The pure panic sent people to the ground to get crushed. Girls screamed, teenagers cried. Chris felt pressed in on all sides. The trees, tents, and vendors created rivers of screaming people. A claustrophobic maze of winding paths. Barely able to breathe, Chris saw people flee into the forest. A surge of bleating announced another avenue of attack.

He felt Stanley lose his grip.

Chris tripped.

He hit the ground.

People kicked him. Stomped him. Clambered over him. He managed to crawl to a knot of bushes where the mob parted. He checked himself. *I'm okay.* His hands felt sticky. He gagged, retracting his hands from the wet vomit on the ground.

He looked around for the others. Unfamiliar people rushed past in a blur, screaming at the top of their lungs. People fell over tents, snapping poles and knocked over carts. Someone kicked up a campfire, sending sparks and coals into a tent.

Fires began to crackle, smoke began to rise, and the braying echoed through the chaos.

He put his head in his hands. *No. No. No. No.* He struggled to breathe. He gripped his chest. *What do I do? What do I do?* He was suffocating. He clawed at his collar. The attack set in. He needed to escape. Escape everything. He searched for something to do that.

Something landed next to him.

A body.

The girl who camped next to them. Her makeup dripped down her cheeks. Her face and body bled from a single slice running from her forehead to her exposed navel. She whimpered. Her blue eyes watering. She was still alive. Blood seeped out everywhere.

Something pressed against her back. A hoof. A black, cloven hoof. Chris's vision followed a leg covered in thick curly fur to a belt hanging off emaciated hips with charms and scalps hooked to a chain.

The branches blocked Chris's view.

All he saw was a pair of curled black horns and a yellow eye with an oblong pupil. It wailed a bleating cry. With a rush of air, an axe blade spit the skull of the girl. Blood splattered Chris's face. Hot iron flooded his senses. He tried not to puke. The creature wrenched the axe free. The rusted steel dripping red.

Her brains leaked between the bloody halves of her shattered skull. Her blue eyes vacant.

Chris crawled backwards.

The hooves turned to his direction. The creature still obscured by the foliage. Chris heard it sniffing for him. He became very aware of how badly he smelled of sweat and booze from two days without a shower.

Gunshots echoed nearby.

The police?

The creature turned back the way it came. Its hooves squishing against the wet ground. It vanished behind trees and tents.

Chris scrambled to his feet. He needed to get out of here. He didn't know where. He just kept moving. He passed more corpses. The mangled bodies of hapless young people. Pink intestines squished under his shoes. An old metalhead with a grey beard clutched the stumps where his legs used to be. He wept for someone named Sam.

Chris vomited by a smoldering campfire. *Keep moving,* he told himself. He paused near a green tent. Trying to control his own breathing. More screams nearby. He smelled smoke. The burning of nylon and bodies. The campsite was on fire.

More gunshots in the distance. He saw flashes towards the parking lot.

The police. Find the police. It made sense. Where else was he supposed to go? They would have working vehicles. They had radios. They had guns.

He headed in the direction of the parking lot. Trying to stay low. He saw people running into the forest. They were pursued by the horned figures. Metal clanged and there was a wet slapping sound. The screaming was all-encompassing. It echoed across the valley. He didn't think the forest was a good idea. They came *from* the forest.

More flashes of gunfire.

Between the gunshots, Chris heard heavy crashes. Footfalls.

He saw something move.

More gunshots.

A towering figure lumbered between the pines. Almost twenty feet tall, almost human shaped, with a pair of long crooked horns sprouting from its head.

More gunshots. This time, in a concentrated burst.

The figure stumbled. It reared its huge head, belting out an earth rumbling roar. Chris covered his ears. It carried what looked like a tree log as a club.

It swung.

Metal crunched.

Red and blue lights flashed. Siren wailing through the air. Chris dove to the side. A police cruiser crashed into the ground. Crumpling its front end. Tents crushed beneath. Clods of dirt exploded from the impact.

He stumbled to his feet.

A cop's broken body hung halfway out of the vehicle. Almost severed at the waist due to the glass shards. Long strings of blood and organs stretching between the halves.

Chris stumbled backwards. *Where do I go? Where do I—*

"Psssst! Jackass, get down," called a familiar voice.

Chris turned. Stanley and the others were there. All of them. They hid between two tents, sheltered by a tarp. Chris crawled towards them.

He saw a bonfire in the distance, closer to the stage. Horned shadows danced around the flames. They waved weapons and torches. Smaller ones waved poles with heads or wriggling body parts impaled to the end. A satanic orgy of fire and blood worship.

Chris dove into his friends before any of the creatures noticed him.

Curt embraced him. "I thought we lost you."

"I thought I lost all of you," said Chris. "How did you manage to stick together?"

"Pure fucking luck," said Lucas. "And Stanley holding us together when we lost you."

"You're covered in blood," said Stanley.

Chris wiped his face with his sleeve. "We need to get

out of here."

"No shit," said Lucas.

Stanley hissed. "Quiet. We need a vehicle."

"They were all sabotaged," said Chris.

"A mechanic was on his way. There might be tools, or maybe just a working vehicle. The police came in cruisers. There might be a working one left."

Everyone nodded.

Except Curt. "You want to run to where the monsters were headed?"

"The monsters are everywhere. We either die waiting here, or we might die trying to escape. We need to risk it."

Curt shook his head. "We should find a place to hide. A place where *they* have already been."

"*They?* Is anyone else wondering that the fuck *they* are?" said Lucas.

"Don't know. Don't care," said Stanley. "We need a vehicle."

Curt shook his head. "You're going to get us all killed."

"Shut up, Curt," spat Stanley. "Your bullshit has brought us enough trouble. I will not let you fuck up this too… not when our lives are at stake."

Curt looked like he'd been slapped.

Stanley moved low to the ground. The others followed, almost crawling. Curt didn't protest. He followed. Screams and bleating echoed in all directions.

They avoided any paths with light. Taking their time to go around the bonfires. They stopped and hid when a parade of heads on pikes passed by with horribly delighted bleating. *What could they want? Just wholesale slaughter?*

Chris kept his focus on moving. *Slow and steady. Slow and steady.* One step at a time. He put one hand in front of the other. The wet ground soaked his knees and hands. Whenever they came to a mangled body, Chris held his breath and shut his eyes. He kept moving.

They came to the edge of the campsite. Hiding behind some bushes.

Stanley waved them over. "Once we find a working car. We won't have much time before they notice."

"What about keys?" said Lucas. "Unless one of you secretly knows how to hotwire a car?"

"Then find something *with* keys, all right? Okay, go." He crept through the bushes and into the parking lot. Chris followed.

They halted.

There were no creatures.

Just bodies.

And crows.

Bodies everywhere. Too many to count. Piled up eight feet high. Blood flecked the neon volunteer vests. Vacant eyes staring at them. Crows pecked at corpses. Narrow beaks full of red sinew. One cried at them before tearing out an eyeball. The blood mixed with the rainwater swirling over the gravel.

A police officer's body lay spread-eagle on the hood of a white Toyota. His ribcage broken open to reveal the insides. The long entrails pulled out and draped around the body in a cyclical pattern. Symbols drawn in blood covered the Toyota.

The cop had his own heart stuffed into his mouth.

Chris heard Lucas vomit behind a bush. Heaving followed by a splatter. Chris would have too if he hadn't already emptied his stomach.

Stanley was green. He clenched his fists, then moved to check the first vehicle.

Chris followed.

They had no choice.

They searched for almost thirty minutes before Chris

found a van with "Larry's Auto" written on the side. He looked through the window. There was no one in the driver's seat. Chris saw the keys hanging from the ignition.

"Guys," he whispered. Waving at Lucas. "Over here."

He tried to open the driver's door. It was locked. Stanley tried. "Let's try the back."

Curt and Lucas gripped the handles of the backdoor. Chris thought he heard noise inside. He wasn't sure if it was just his imagination or not. The others felt the same. Stanley nodded to the other two. They all tensed as the doors opened.

In the back of the vehicle were racks of tools and a body. An overweight mechanic lay dead in a pool of his own blood. His overalls red and his round face frozen in a grimace of horror. His throat opened up with jagged bite marks.

Hunched over him was a child, or rather, in the shape of a child. A bald, oversized head, thin arms, a bloated stomach. Its legs were crooked, furry, and hooved, and from its forehead grew two stubby horns.

It looked up from its feast. Its mouth of tiny sharp teeth dripping in blood. It blinked with whiteless eyes. The four young men were frozen, horrified. It opened its mouth to scream and signal the rest of the monsters.

Chris acted on instinct. His body already past the point of shock. He reacted. He grabbed a screwdriver on the floor and thrust it into the child-thing's throat. Its scream reduced to a gurgle before it had a chance. It clawed at his arm. Its nails digging into his sleeve. He slammed it against the side of a toolbox. He felt its body shudder still.

He stumbled back, almost falling. Curt caught him. They stared at him with more horror and surprise than the sight of the massacre. "Let's get the fuck out of here," said Chris.

Stanley and Chris climbed in and rolled the bodies out and onto the ground with a disgusted grimace. Lucas ran around to the hood. Curt kept watch. Stanley popped the hood; Lucas checked to make sure everything was in order.

As they waited. Stanley turned to Chris. "Are you—"

"I'm fine, Stan. Please."

"I just saw you kill something like it was nothing. You acted before any of us could even blink. You…"

"Drop it," said Chris. His hands were trembling with shock. He steeled himself. Why had he been able to do that? How had he been able to do that? He reacted. *I guess I had been thinking about death. All the ways someone can die…* He had just never meant it for anyone else.

The worst part was…

It felt good. He had saved his friends.

He rubbed his head, then realized he had just smeared blood on his face. He wiped it with his sleeve. "You think we can get out of this?" he asked.

Stanley shrugged, fingers gripping the keys.

Lucas shut the hood as quietly as he could. He gave them a thumbs up.

Everyone piled in, avoiding the pool of blood on the floor. Stanley and Chris looked back at the others. They nodded.

"Let's get the fuck out of here," said Stanley.

He looked forward.

A crow stood on the hood. Its beady black eyes focused on them. It cocked its head and cried at them.

Stanley turned the key. The moment lasted an eternity. All the ways they would die flooded into Chris's mind. It would be easier to slit their wrists before they let the creatures get them. They had all these sharp tools in the van. It would be fast.

It clicked, and the engine rumbled to life. The crow scattered.

Yes. They all exhaled.

The lights only further illuminated the massacre. The piles of bodies. The bloody symbols and ritually arranged corpses.

Stanley didn't say anything; his jaw was clenched. He pressed the gas. Bodies crunched under the tires. They couldn't avoid them. They didn't have the time. Every crunch sent chills up Chris's spine. They escape the blood-soaked parking lot and managed to get on to the road.

Lucas watched the road behind them. Nothing followed.

They drove in silence.

◆

Chris watched the trees go by. The moon cracked through the cloud cover. It was full. A pale, sickly green bathing the forest road in ghostly light. He wondered if it had anything to do with this. The ritualized murders, the massacre, the bonfire of horrors. It all seemed like things monsters would connect to the moon.

"You think Tracy and the others are okay?" asked Curt.

Stanley glanced in the rearview mirror with a flat expression.

Curt looked at his feet. He leaned against a toolbox. They all knew the answer.

"Do you think anyone knows?" said Lucas. "Someone

has to know about those… things. The government, the CIA, the Church? Someone?"

"Government probably let it happen," said Curt.

"To what end?" said Stanley. "Kill a bunch of taxpayers? Control us more? Test a weapon? Keep the conspiracy theories to yourself. If someone actually knew, none of this would have happened." He looked at Curt for a while.

Curt saw it. "You're such a pretentious asshole…"

"Guilty."

"Fuck you, Stan. People are dying!"

"Yeah, and I *said* we should have left hours ago. We might have escaped this…"

"So, it's my fault!" Curt barked, his face getting red.

Stanley sighed. "No. It's not. You did not cause monsters to fucking leap out of the forest and start slaughtering people. You didn't cause the rain, or the food, or any of it… but we wouldn't have stayed if it wasn't for you."

Curt glared.

Chris looked down… *No. It's my fault.* Chris had said they should go back for the one final show. They might have avoided all of this. *It's my fault…* He should have just been taken by the monsters.

Chris looked up. He didn't even have a chance to scream.

They hit something hard. Tools went flying. A wrench slammed into the windshield. Cracking the glass. The airbags exploded. Chris bounced back, smacked against the headrest. Shards of glass glanced off his face. He looked at Stanley, even with the pain shooting up his neck and into his brain. Stanley groaned, a dozen cuts across his face and arms. A few more groans behind them. Chris strained to check.

They're okay.

Curt was flat on the floor, rubbing his head, which had smacked against a toolbox. *I knew he had a thick head.* Lucas was okay too. He covered his head with his arms.

Then he looked forward.

Only one headlight worked, so it was only half illuminated. A huge form rose into view. It had been shoved by the van. A massive cloven hoof clacked against the gravel. Steam poured from its drooling maw.

Its axe had slid down the road. A blade of steel the size of a doorframe covered in dried blood. Its tree trunk handle was broken in half. The creature looked at its broken weapon. It was easily six feet wide at the shoulders, fur running down its back. It barely had a neck, just a trunk of solid muscle. It grunted, then turned its huge head back to the vehicle.

Tiny black eyes shadowed by huge bullhorns. Sharp and curled forward. Its maw dripped with strings of drool. It bared its bear-like teeth. Its snout shot jets of steam. It got up. Both legs covered in thick matted fur, crooked, and ending in wide, sprawled out hoofs. Around its waist hung pelts and freshly severed human heads. Their faces full of shock and terror.

It roared.

Chris slapped his hands over his ears.

It charged. Horns first.

The van bucked backwards. Everyone yelled. Stanley came to his senses. He slammed on the gas. The tires screeched. The monster reared its huge head. It snarled, pushing against the van with its immense muscled mass, clawed hands crumpling the hood. Stanley pushed harder. Curt and the others yelled, "Get it! Come on!"

The wheels smoked. The creature roared, its tiny black eyes full of blind rage. Saliva splattered against the windshield. It lowered its horns, breaking through the glass. Stanley screamed. He turned the wheel. The creature lost its grip. It pushed its horns forward.

Chris met Stanley's eyes.

One horn went straight through Stanley's neck with a wet crunch. His voice croaked as blood seeped over his chest.

Chris screamed.

The monster lifted the front end of the van. Its chest heaved. It tossed the van on its side. Everyone inside screamed as they were thrown against the wall of the van. Metal crunched against gravel. Chris, hanging in his seat, saw the creature's huge hooves stomping towards them.

Chris undid his seatbelt. He felt a strong arm grip him. Curt's arm. He looked at Stanley, the wound in his neck left his head hanging limp, only connected by a few strands of flesh. Blood pouring down onto Chris's face.

It was all a blur. The noise. The roaring.

Next thing he knew, Curt dragged him out the back of the van. Lucas limped towards the edge of the road. *Stanley's gone.* The creature roared.

Curt dragged Chris who protested, "We can't leave him!"

"We have to!"

Chris turned. The monster reached into the van, the light shining behind it. Its horn dripped with blood. *No.* It pulled Stanley's body out of the wreckage. Glass broke against the ground. His head hung limp. *No.* It gripped his waist and his legs. *No!* It pulled him apart like a toy. *NO!*

They reached the woods. Chris's view of the monster blocked. All he heard was its triumphant roar and wet smacking sounds.

♦

They stopped by a rock. Deep within the forest. Trees rose around them like a barrier but offered no comfort. The roars had disappeared in the distance after a while. The following silence was haunting. No birds, no insects, just the endless ambience of the forest.

Chris limped along. He couldn't feel his legs. Curt helped Lucas to the ground. A shard of glass protruded from Lucas's shin.

Lucas howled. "What the fuck was that thing?!" He clutched his arm; some wires and metal components stuck out of it. Blood dripped down his elbow. Curt kneeled, helping pluck the objects from Lucas's flesh. Lucas swore each time. Curt tore a strip off his shirt and wrapped Lucas's arm before getting to work on the glass in his leg.

"I don't know," said Curt.

Chris looked at his hands. They shook. He worked the feeling back into his legs. His head hurt. Everything hurt… *Stanley's gone. Oh, God. He's really gone.* A panic began to set in. Chris couldn't do this without Stanley. He couldn't do anything without Stanley. He needed him. *A lot more than he needed me.*

What do I tell his family?

Chris couldn't get the image out of his mind. The monster tearing Stanley in half. He couldn't even vomit or cry. Everything was just numb. *I can't do this.* He needed a way out.

Chris couldn't get up. They should leave him here. Just let them find him. How could he go home? How could he face Stanley's family? They were like his second parents. They had begged Stanley to go with Chris. They were there when he was in the hospital. How could—

"Hey." Curt shook Chris's shoulders. "Are you okay?"

"What?"

"Are. You. O-kay?"

Chris re-centered himself. "I think so."

"Good." Curt stood up. "We gotta go. We need to find a place to hide."

"Hide?!" barked Lucas. "Where the fuck can we hide from those?!"

"We ran into that thing because Stanley said we should run. We *had* to run. He *had* to be right. Look what fucking happened!"

Chris got to his feet. Anger pumping over the shock. "He's dead."

Curt frowned. Only ashamed enough to know how it sounded, not enough to really think he was wrong. Curt was bleeding above his left eye. He wiped it away. "We have to—"

"HELP!" cried a woman's voice.

They all froze. The cry came again. *It's close.* Curt helped Lucas to his feet. They all hobbled towards the source of the voice. It was over the next ridge.

"HELP! Is anyone out there?"

They neared the ridge. A girl wandered through a gully in the forest. She was boxed in by rocks. She had herself trapped. She clutched her arm; it was broken. Her cheeks covered in ruined makeup. Red hair in a mess. Her clothes torn.

"That's Tracy's roommate," said Curt. He got up on the ridge. Chris's eyes went wide. He grabbed Curt by his shirt and pulled him back down. Chris barked in a hushed voice. "Stay down."

"What? She needs help!"

Chris pulled Curt down and pointed to the entrance to

the gully. Something moved. Something big.

"We can't help her," said Chris. His heart jumped into his throat. He knew how wrong it was, but Stanley died trying to get them to safety. They couldn't just get themselves killed. One minute, Curt was begging them to hide. The next, he was ready to rush in to help someone. Maybe that was his admirable trait?

Lucas hobbled behind a tree. "He's right. We should go. Head towards town."

"Help!" she cried, her voice hoarse. "Help me!"

Curt's eyes darted back and forth. "Screw this! We have to help her." He got up. Chris grabbed him. Clapping his hand over Curt's mouth. His body running on nothing but adrenaline and fear. Lucas joined in, falling into the scuffle. Curt was pinned against the ground. He was bigger than either of them, but not both of them.

Movement crashed through the forest. Hooves echoed, clattering against the stone, then splashing in the gully. The girl shrieked. Her own splashes were smaller. Then she stopped. More hooves followed from the other direction. *There were two.* There could have been more.

She whimpered, begging, pleading for her life. As if these creatures understood. Curt struggled against his friends. Lucas watched helplessly. Chris whispered in

Curt's ear. "There's two. You think we can take two? In our condition? We need to leave."

The girl cried. The creatures made a deep throaty sound. *Are they laughing?* There was no whoosh of a sword or axe. They just laughed. There was a thunk and a splash. The girl shrieked, crying louder.

Defeat set into Curt's eyes. He knew they were right.

The monsters laughed.

They were toying with her.

Hooves splashed. She cried.

We have to get out of here.

Clothing ripped.

Oh, no.

Chris got off Curt. They gathered Lucas and headed north, towards town. They left, leaving the screaming and monstrous laughter behind them. It rung across the forest. Destroying any semblance of hope Chris had for their survival. He would never be able to unhear those sounds. They abandoned that girl to her fate and the mercy of those monsters.

Chris felt he was becoming another monster with each step.

♦

They walked in silence.

They took turns helping Lucas walk. They were exhausted, hungry and dehydrated, and maybe still a little hungover. Chris hurt all over.

After an hour, they found a creek. Curt kept watch from a rocky outcropping.

Chris was so thirsty he fell to his knees and shoved his whole face in the ice-cold water. It stung his cheeks. It felt good. He lapped it up. He jumped when he saw blood drifting down the stream, then he realized it was Stanley's blood washing off his face.

The roar and wet snap replayed in his brain. He sat back, feeling the ache in his legs. His knees soaked. He rubbed the whiplash in his neck.

Lucas climbed down for a quick drink. He washed his arm and mumbled about tetanus. Unable to get up on his injured leg. The glass stuck out of his leg. They needed a doctor to remove it. They wrapped it in his plaid button-up as best they could.

"You'll be fine," growled Chris.

"Shut up," hissed Lucas.

Chris flipped him off. No joke in it at all. Lucas pulled

out his phone, the only one they had. "Still can't get *anything*, fucking useless."

"Put it away! We'll need it later!" said Curt.

"Quiet!" hissed Chris. He stopped feeling any fear. He didn't care to hide anymore. He just didn't care anymore. It wasn't worth the effort.

"We need to keep moving," said Curt, trying to break the tension.

"What's the fucking point," barked Lucas. "We're going to die."

"No, we won't!" said Curt. "We need a place to hide. If we wait long enough, help will come."

"Hiding won't work," said Chris. "If we hide, we're just surrendering to those *things*. We'll just be waiting to die. If we run, then we have a fucking chance." *Am I really saying that?*

"You're going to get us killed! We need to hide!"

Chris was on his feet. "All you ever do is hide! If we hide, we die!"

"Will you two be quiet?" hissed Lucas. "You want them to hear you?"

Curt lowered his voice. "Don't you start acting all high and mighty too. Chris, you avoid everything. You ignore and run from everything. Don't act like you're better than me... Don't..."

"Act like Stanley?"

Curt blinked. "Yeah."

"He was right. We need to actually try and escape. Hiding gives *them* all the power. It's quitting. I am done trying to quit." He had been in the hospital for a reason. He'd tried to quit once before. He wouldn't do that anymore.

"How'd that work out for him?"

Stanley's blood still stained their clothes. Chris clenched his fists. "About as unlucky as anyone could be."

"That daddy's boy had everything on a silver platter. He never knew how we felt."

Chris stepped forward. "And now he's dead. All that luck you were jealous of finally ran out. He took the risk. He *tried.* Something you've never done." Chris jabbed his finger into Curt's chest. "Everything he said about you is true."

Curt glowered, standing taller and larger than Chris. "We're going to find a place to hide. I won't let you get us all killed."

Chris didn't care anymore.

He couldn't stand the sight of Curt. His round face,

greasy beard, and tiny black eyes. Most of all the sad, hurt eyes and the confused look he had when he couldn't understand why Chris didn't want to party. He guilted them all for their inadequate amount of sympathy.

He walked away. Heading north, towards town. He had had enough. Even if he was alone. He already felt alone. It didn't matter. He…

He heard uneven footsteps behind him.

Lucas limped along to join him. "Let's go," said Lucas, almost like he needed to convince himself.

The pair continued through the dark sentinel pines. They left Curt alone, stumbling like a lost child without his parents. He was alone, and the last thing Chris saw of him was him falling to his knees, burying his hands in his face and sobbing.

♦

They hobbled north. Avoiding major hiking trails and paths. It was rough. Especially with Lucas's leg. They tried to be quiet. Sneaking through the bush. They didn't know what could be listening.

After a while, Lucas broke the total silence. "Do you think we're near town?"

"We have to be," said Chris. Holding a branch so Lucas

could get through.

Lucas met Chris's eye. "You were pretty harsh to Curt."

"Good, he needed to hear it."

"Yeah," said Lucas. "For a long time."

"You were fed up with him too?" asked Chris.

"Uh huh, he was such a brat. Blamed it on his parents, on his brother, on Liza. When he got drunk, which was always, he blamed it on Stanley too."

"For what?" said Chris.

"For being superior."

"He wasn't. He was our friend. He always shared with us and always wanted to help. Life was just messy for the rest of us." Chris snorted. "Immaturity really does come from insecurity."

"Yeah," said Lucas.

A pause.

Lucas looked up. "Chloe broke up with me…"

Chris felt like they all already knew.

Silence.

Chris snorted. "Over text?" Lucas nodded. "What a fucking bitch. Didn't event respect you enough to do it in person?"

Chris saw a smile creep over Lucas's face. "Yeah, she was probably fucking Gerald too... They hung out last week. It seemed weird. I pretended I didn't know what was happening. Even after she threw a fit for me hanging out with Tessa, who's like my goddamn sister."

"Gerald Chang?"

"Yeah," sighed Lucas. "I once saw him shirtless at a gay club. Probably just seeing her to convince his parents, and himself, that he isn't gay."

Chris laughed. "Wait... wait... what were you doing in a gay club?"

"Sister's birthday. She picked the bar that looked fun."

"What were you doing at your sister's birthday?" teased Chris.

Chris hoisted Lucas over a log. "I happen to have a good relationship with my family. I love my baby sister." Lucas looked up. "Chris, I just want to see my sister again." His voice cracked. "That's all I want. I could go to jail. I could be killed. I just want to see my sister again. Please. We have to get out of here."

"We will."

They carried on through the forest... that is... until

they smelled smoke.

No.

It drifted through the trees, a heavy thick air, coming from the north over the next ridge. They hurried. Chris pulled branches out of the way. A heavy glow broke through the underbrush.

They broke the treeline.

Chris froze.

Lucas sat on the ground and buried his face in his hands.

Numbness took Chris.

The town, Brenton, was on fire. Businesses and houses engulfed in flames. Shadows dancing their macabre rituals of death and slaughter. The square was a ring of torches and stakes. The statue of the town's founder was broken and replaced with a totem of black ashen wood. A tall, horned glyph of some primordial god.

In the square was a huge bonfire. The tips of the flames reaching high above the buildings. Bodies were impaled on the stakes around the circle. More monsters danced back and forth. There was a rhythm to the chanting and bleating. Others stood over screaming victims sacrificing their hearts and entrails.

The monsters would take turns scrawling symbols on the bloated pregnant bellies of she-beasts and their other monstrous mates. Monsters conceived a new generation of horrors covered in the blood of humans. The bleating was a demonic chorus beyond anything Chris could possibly have ever imagined.

Cackling crows perched on every roof and post, screaming encouragement. Blood seeped across the cobblestone, reflecting the firelight.

The concert had been nothing; a sideshow. In the center of this picture of hell stood a single silhouetted monster. Perfectly muscled, standing tall on its oversized goat legs. An axe and curved blade in either hand. Two pairs of horns sprouted from its head in a star-like arrangement.

It raised its weapons, braying into the night before beheading another victim. The whole town responded with a chorus of bleating, shrieking, and roaring. Another giant shadow farther into the town broke a building in half.

More human screams followed. More violent than ever.

"We need to go," said Chris.

Lucas nodded after a long pause.

They ran–hobbled–back into the forest.

♦

The forest still smelled of smoke and blood. Fleets of crows flew towards the town. Chris stumbled along with Lucas leaning on him. They weaved through a hiking trail. His legs had stopped aching. Now it was just putting one foot in front of the other. *One foot in front of the other. One foot in front of the other.*

There must have been a ranger station or something. Someone must know. Someone had to know.

"Morning should be soon, right?" He couldn't tell who said it. He had no idea what time it was.He didn't even know where they were. Or where they were headed. Had they been trying to circle widely around the town? Had they been searching for a highway to get help? Were they headed north until they found the next town? All Chris knew was he had to put one foot in front of the other. *One foot—*

"Sweet Caroline!" echoed through the trees.

Chris whipped around. Lucas pulled out his phone, eyes wide. "It's Chloe!"

"Shut it off!" barked Chris.

Lucas answered the phone, bouncing on his good leg. "Baby! I'm sorry. I am so sorry. You know I didn't mean it. I—"

The call ended, cut out by the reception again. "Fuck!"

hissed Lucas as he fiddled with the phone.

There was a rustle. Chris turned and was knocked to the ground. His head rung. Lucas was knocked over next to him.

Someone, a person, picked up the phone off the ground. Chris blinked, clearing his vision.

Three of the skinhead punks from the festival stood over them. They were just as bloodied and injured as Chris and Lucas. One had an arm in a sling, another had a gash over his eyes and nursed a bad limp. The middle one, the one who had been harassing Chris, had a gash down his face, blue eyes ringed with red. His *The Base* T-shirt was splattered with blood. In his hand he carried a crude sabre.

A sabre from one of the monsters. It looked like a long fang of rusted steel with a grip wrapped in leather.

He held up the phone. "Thanks." His pale face stretched with a half-insane smile. He looked down on Chris. Eyes were filled with complete contempt. Chris grit his teeth. He wanted to slash that sword across the fascist's face. *They're no better than the monsters.*

Humans no better than beasts.

They turned to walk away, taking the phone. The one with a limp stopped. "Hey." He glanced at Chris with the eyes like a wild animal. "You know this'll be the only chance we can ever have."

The other two looked at Chris. They were wolves. Wolves who had found their favourite prey just waiting. Chris tried to crawl back. Lucas tried to do the same.

"Yeah," said the leader. "You're right. Who's gonna know?"

The one in a sling grabbed a heavy stick like a truncheon. The one with a limp pulled out a butterfly knife. They all stalked back towards Chris. They would kill him first. After running from monsters, it was going to be humans that killed Chris.

They moved to lunge.

Something snapped. The air hissed. With a wet *thunk*, a black arrow struck the skinhead in the chest. The phone slipped from his fingers. He touched the arrow shaft as red seeped down his shirt. He collapsed.

Chris yelled wordlessly.

"Get down!" barked Lucas

Chris sprawled. The skinheads scattered, arrows zipped through the air. Chris tried to reach for the phone. *Someone has to know.* He crawled towards the device; the blue glow bathed the clearing.

He reached.

"No! Get off me!" screamed Lucas.

Chris touched the phone. It lost the signal.

A black hoof crushed the phone into the dirt with a metallic crunch.

Chris's hand shot back. He tried to look up. A hoof slammed into his face. Pain exploded through his skull. His vision went blurry. He tasted blood.

Rough hands grabbed his ankles and shoulders. They dragged him away. He blinked through the tears. Lucas was being dragged away too. Two of the skinheads lay dead.

The creatures went for the bodies. They were short, stocky, and naked except for maybe a belt or loincloth. They were goatish below the waist. Above, they had tanned shoulders like any other person. Some bald, some had thick matted hair.

Horns sprout from their foreheads. They attacked the bodies in a frenzy. Growling in some animalistic language. They stripped away the punk's clothes and remaining possessions. One raised an axe. A wet clap was followed by the whole pack screaming in approval. One raised the severed head. His jaw hanging frozen in his final look of confusion. Blood dripped from the neck. Tears still seeped from his eyes.

Chris screamed long and loud. A fist with hairy knuckles sent Chris into darkness.

He dreamt of blood and screaming. He saw the massacre and the sacrifices. The burning town. He saw the face and felt the death shudder of the child-monster he killed. He saw Stanley impaled by horns and torn in half. He heard the girl screaming for help. Then the tearing of clothing. He saw the skinheads going after him. He saw Curt being abandoned in the forest, alone and confused. He saw *them;* their hooves, their horns, their blood crazed bleating.

Then he was in a hospital bed. His mom was asleep in a chair next to him. His dad couldn't face him. Not for what he had written in his goodbye note. He thought he had made sure it would be successful. He thought he could finally escape from everything. The anxiety, the mistakes, the failings, the expectations, the disappointment.

He just wanted to escape. So, he put a razor to his wrists and pulled.

It had failed.

Now everyone knew how broken he really was.

Now everyone knew how weak he really was.

Now everyone knew how selfish he really was.

Now he would never be able to escape again, because

everyone would be watching him.

He was exactly what they saw him as; weak, pathetic, fragile, and a disappointment.

♦

He was woken by the reek of burnt hair and smoke.

His head throbbed. His lips crusted with his own clotted blood. He felt warmth on his face from a nearby fire. He cracked opened his eyes. Firelight flooded his vision. He groaned, pushing himself up. The ground shook with rhythmic pounding, like the beating of a great drum. The pounding in his head matched its tempo.

He spat up over the cobblestone.

His senses focused and he looked up.

He felt his stomach sink. *They* were everywhere.

They surrounded the town square in a picture of bestial fury. Tall ones, short ones, ones with horns, a few without. The smallest looked like humans with large noses and floppy ears, lacking horns, screeching like they were on helium. The majority were those bleating goat-things. Some had human faces which only made their horns, hooves, and snarling teeth more disturbing. Many had a muzzle like a goat but with jagged wolf teeth, or even a tusked piggish face.

Huge ones like the one on the highway roared, beating their chests, stomping their hooves. There were ones with a horse's body with a man or a goat-thing's torso, or just a human face, delighted by the rape and slaughter. Ones with extra arms, others with one eye instead of two. A dozen more horrible mutants beyond description scattered through the horde.

He noticed that many were female, distinguished by their heavy sagging teats and round pregnant bellies covered in swirling symbols drawn in blood. Around their necks hung gifts of fingers, ears, toes, and severed genitals.

The ground shook with meteoric footfalls. A pair of giants stood at opposite sides of the square. One looked like the bull-things but twenty-feet tall. Its long horns spread out horizontally from its head. Around its hairy waist hung a dozen people. Dead, mutilated, and dangling by their necks. The other giant looked human, except for the thick horns sprouting from its temples and the single bulbous eye in the middle of its forehead. It chewed on the back half of a cow. Its enormous maw crunched and dripped in liquid.

The crows circled above. Drunk on their endless feast of flesh. They cackled as loudly as the monsters.

That's when Chris realized he wasn't alone. He was surrounded by other survivors. Some were still unconscious. Others, like Chris, were only just pushing through their delirium. A few were on their feet.

Chris thought he recognized a few. Another skinhead from the concert, but this one was less concerned with Chris than his friends were. There was the grocery store owner, still wearing his smock, only now splattered with blood. The girl Curt had bought drugs from. Glitter and makeup smeared. Lucas was next to Chris. He sat up, and his leg looked even worse. Gushing pus and coagulated blood.

"Oh, my God," said Lucas.

Another stood up, Curt, his face bruised and bloodied, but otherwise okay. He didn't look at Chris or Lucas. He stared at the monsters, fists clenched. He was shaking, his fists clenched. *We abandoned him,* thought Chris, horror and guilt spreading through his chest.

One entered the square. The chorus of roars and bleats intensified, growing deafening. The stomping shook the ground.

The lone creature was enormous, powerful. Almost seven feet tall with arms and torso like an Olympian. Its four horns in a parody of a star. Its thick neck covered with a mane of matted fur. On its waist hung a large brass pentagram with chains hooked with more grizzly trophies. It had a long scar running across its muzzle. It bared its sharp teeth. *A smile.* It raised its hand.

Silence.

Every single monster and crow stood frozen. Chris looked around. They didn't even seem to breathe. They stared intensely at the survivors. The remaining few got to their feet.

The lone creature, the chieftain, watched the humans. Its oblong pupils were not wild with animal instinct. They were focused, perceptive, and calculating. He stepped closer to the survivors, leering over them. He smiled again and grunted something indecipherable.

A few dozen of the smallest imps and goat-thing runts rushed to the survivors. People screamed, people tried to run, but it didn't work. They were everywhere. Chris didn't bother.

Their little fingers gripped their clothing. They tore away their shirts and pants. Everyone was stripped to their underwear. The female survivors were stripped as bare-chested as the men. Chris knew he couldn't fight it. They tore off his shirt, revealing the bandages around his wrists. The scars on his thighs and shoulders. Lucas was shoved to his feet. He limped horribly, unable to put any weight on that bad leg.

Chris helped him stand. "Curt! Help me!"

Curt ignored them.

The grocer helped hold up Lucas, his eyes wide with fear. "What is going on?"

More small creatures ran into the square. They deposited weapons at everyone's feet. They shoved axes, mauls, sickles, swords, and blades of all kinds into everyone's hands. The skinhead gripped his axe. He wanted to live. They all wanted to live. They all formed into groups, back-to-back, against the horde of monsters.

That doesn't make any sense. They wouldn't give the survivors weapons just to kill them. These creatures had no code of honour. They wouldn't have slaughtered the way they did if they had. They wouldn't give them a fighting chance to survive the onslaught. *Oh, no.*

The chieftain laughed, shaking its monstrous head.

The skinhead charged the chieftain, axe raised. "Die, you fucker!"

The chieftain dodged the swing, moving far more fluidly than his mass should allow. He grabbed the punk by the throat. He threw the skinhead against the ground.

The punk wheezed, coughing up blood. The chieftain raised its hoof and brought it down on the punk's head. Crunching it like a melon. Blood, brain, and skull fragments gushed over the ground. The survivors shrieked.

The chieftain laughed, shaking its head again. It loomed over the survivors like a demonic god of the wilds. "Fight," it said. Its rough voice gurgled the words like the language couldn't fit its lips. Several survivors gasped in disbelief. "Fight. Fight, winner leaves." It raised its hand again. The monsters separated, making a path northward.

The survivors froze. They knew exactly what it meant.

Won't they just kill us anyways? Chris held a curved sword. What was he supposed to do? He had to get Lucas out of here. He had to get Curt out of here. He had—

Curt turned, raised his double-bladed battle axe, and brought it down on a girl's head. Cleaving her in half. Blood splattering his round face.

The monsters exploded into roaring cheers. The rhythm of bleating and stomping resumed.

The survivors turned on each other in an instant. Blades biting into naked bodies. The glittery girl leapt into an older man's arms, smashing a cleaver into his face. Others wrestled to the ground, smashing faces into the cobblestone. A teenager spilled his friend's intestines with a rusted sword.

The violence of the attack, seeing everyone killed so brutally, the trauma and horror of it all had turned them into killers. Desperate to survive, they had become animals. Exposed to such complete violence forced them to embrace that very horror.

The grocer looked at Lucas and Chris, eyes full of regret. "I'm sorry." He raised the blade in his hand.

Chris reacted on instinct, shoving his own blade into the grocer's chest. Lucas punched the pencil-lipped man, sending him to the ground. They hobbled away from the massacre. A large woman with drooping breasts confronted them, her arms shaking as she raised a spiked club. Chris shoved Lucas to the side. The club broke against the ground.

The woman shrieked, "Wait! I'm sorry! I'm sorry!"

Chris couldn't hesitate. He slashed the woman in the face. She fell to the ground clutching her eyes, screaming.

He ran to Lucas but was attacked by the teenager who split his own friend. He thrust a blade at Chris. Chris raised his arm. The blade pierced his forearm, pain exploded up to his shoulder. He grunted. Blood seeped into his bandages.

Not the first time I've felt a blade in my arm. He used his impaled arm to hold the blade. Then he brought his own blade down, cleaving off the teenager's arm.

Chris kicked the flailing teenager away. He groaned as he pulled the sword from his arm.

He looked up. The chieftain smiled, he looked so smug and self-satisfied. As if he was proving a point.

"Chris!"

He turned, Lucas was on the ground, using a broken club to fend off the young woman with the cleaver. Her face covered in red. Eyes wild with blood frenzy.

Chris slammed into her. They tumbled, she snarled, trying to hit him with the cleaver. He pinned her arm with his bleeding wrist. She bit down on his bloodied bandages. If a sword couldn't phase him, neither would teeth. He gripped her head with his good arm and smashed it against the cobblestone. Again and again and again.

He stood up. Her face frozen in the desperate snarl. Eyes wild. Chris's legs shook. *What have we become?*

"Chris!"

He turned. Bone crunched beneath metal.

Curt stood over Lucas, the axe buried deep in Lucas's chest. His ribcage shattered. Blood poured from his mouth.

Chris yelled in protest. He charged, crashing into Curt. Curt was a wall of fat and muscle, but he was off balance. They both tumbled. Rolling on the cobblestone.

Chris got to his feet, grabbing an axe with spikes on the back of the blade. He looked around. There were no survivors standing. Many weeping, screaming, and dying. It was only Curt and Chris left. They'd all killed one another. The monsters roared in celebration.

The chieftain raised its hand again. Perfect silence, with only the wind and the crackle of the fires.

The chieftain spoke, but only for Curt and Chris. "Fight. Winner leaves."

Chris felt numb. There was no way they wouldn't just kill the winner at the end of this. *Right?* Curt's eyes were distant and detached. Curt wasn't really *here* anymore. Chris was certain that his old friend would cave his skull in. He knew there wasn't any hope for survival. But... maybe they didn't have to murder each other.

"Curt, I'm sorry."

Curt didn't move.

"Curt, I'm sorry I was such a bad friend. We have both been in such dark places. Maybe we could have gotten better together," said Chris. "I know you've been through so much pain. I know what it's like. Feeling like there's no way out except oblivion." *Whether booze or a razor.*

Curt bared his bloodied teeth. Raising his own axe, ready to charge. *He's trembling.*

The chieftain chuckled. "You no different than us." He struggled with the words. "Smell blood, hunt. Taste blood, gorge. Fight, kill. Kill, kill more. Abandoned, revenge." He struggled more with the next word. "Civ-i-liz-a-tion… is lie. Not real. All the men-things are just beasts-inside-lies. Now, kill. Winner will leave."

Chris clutched his axe, he pleaded. "Curt, help me kill this thing. Let's take the only chance we can." Curt didn't move. "They'll pay for this. Let's kill this monster and spit in their eye before we get torn apart."

Curt's vacant expression didn't change.

"Curt, please. Don't let these things control us." He changed tactics. "Don't let Liza keep controlling you. I'm sorry we left you. I'm sorry we abandoned you so many times."

"Shut up," hissed Curt.

"No. She destroyed you, but you're still letting her control you. I've been doing the same. I've let my parents and my grades control me. It isn't all I am. What Liza made you is not you."

"You don't know anything! Not you! Not my dad! Not my brother! Not Stanley! None of you care about me!"

"Did you ever actually know what you felt? Did you?"

Curt didn't move.

"Come on, man. You let Liza control you for so long. You just filled the void with more poison. You *needed* to be a mess to keep from facing the pain. You *needed* to be a disaster and drag all of us with you."

"What was I supposed to do?!"

Chris lowered his axe, the creatures squawked in protest. "You keep blaming everyone, but we all have our own lives. I'm sorry I abandoned you. I'm sorry I left you alone." He sighed. "I had my own demons. I was trapped. I should have gotten help. I should have talked to someone. I should have talked to you. I just felt like I was letting everyone down… I'm sorry."

"I'm sorry too…" said Curt. He glanced at the creatures. "But I ain't letting you stop me from going home." He raised his weapon.

Chris balked. "You think they will really let you leave if you kill me?! Look at them!"

Curt didn't blink.

Chris gripped his own axe in both hands. "Gotta at least try, right?" His arm bled, dripping down his wrist.

Curt charged, screaming, axe over his head. He was so big. He had always been stronger than Chris. He had no chance.

Chris exhaled. He raised the weapon over his head. He let his drained muscles loosen. The axe felt so heavy. *Need to take control of my own life.* Even if it destroyed someone as broken as himself.

He lobbed the axe.

It spun through the air end-over-end and, with a hard, wet crunch, slammed into Curt's chest, just below his throat. Curt's face contorted in pain and confusion. He stumbled. Then collapsed. He fell right next to Lucas's broken body.

The monsters exploded into roaring cheers. They shrieked and cackled with glee. Many danced, leaping and skipping on hoofed feet.

Chris fell to his knees.

The chieftain stepped closer. Towering over Chris. It placed an encouraging hand on his shoulder. It reeked like a zoo cage. It patted his shoulder. "Good. You good. Kill. Not man. Just beast. Liar skin gone. Just beast." It laughed.

The worst part was… Chris knew it was right. He had gone from being broken by fear and anxiety to killing creatures, abandoning people to a fate worse than death, and killing his own friends. He had become something else. Something worse. Something monstrous.

"You go now. Make gods happy." It gripped his shoulder. "Make gods happy." *NO!* Chris tried to run, but the leader's grip was too strong.

Chris tried to reach for a sword, but the chieftain kicked away the nearest weapon. It grinned with its disgusting jagged teeth. It grasped him by the hair and began dragging him towards the totem that had replaced the town's statue.

The glow of the morning licked the edge of the mountains.

Chris tried to crawl away. He tried to fight his way out. He kicked and struggled against the chieftain, but the monster just laughed. "No fight. Make gods happy. Blood makes gods happy. Happy gods, strong cubs, strong calves. Herd goes on."

The circle of monsters collapsed into chaos. Roars and screams shattered the early dawn. Many tore into the corpses of the survivors, making fresh trophies, mutilating corpses. It didn't matter if the survivor was already dead or still dying.

The horde surrounded the totem. A great wooden pillar in the visage of an angry bulbous goat. Its half-dozen pairs of horns twisted, and with its narrow face it created a huge pentagram.

Chris was surrounded. No creature stood in the chieftain's way. They cheered. Screaming and bleating in celebration.

At the foot of the totem was a she-beast. She wore a cloak of raven feathers, only her fat belly covered in bloody glyphs was visible. Her face hidden by a dark hood. A series of horns split through the fabric. Great glassy black horns, all reaching upwards.

Her hands crossed in front of her belly. A long, curved razor in her hands.

The statue's broken torso lay on the ground. Bronze and covered in demonic etchings.

Chris's heart pounded in his chest. The chieftain's grip was too strong. Not like he could even get away. The chieftain slammed him against the bronze altar. Chris was completely surrounded. He wanted to live. He needed to escape.

No chance of it. The leader shoved him against the chest of the statue. He smiled. *I want to live.* Funny how he had to see all his friends die and be sacrificed to learn that. Everything that he had let destroy himself and his life didn't mean much in the end.

If I can't live, then I will die on my terms.

The she-beast neared him with the knife. The chieftain held Chris down with a hand on the back of his head. He just needed to wait. He needed an instant. The gleam of the blade's razor edge. She was going to saw off his head.

The blade was inches from his neck.

Now!

His arm shot out to grab the blade.

He was too slow.

The chieftain snatched his wrist and slammed it against the bronze statue. Pain shot up his arm. The chieftain wrenched him back. Holding him immobile by the neck and arm. It laughed in Chris's ear, breath like rotten flesh. "Little man, too slow. Die now."

The she-beast brought the blade closer. The horde of creatures roared in approval. The climax of their orgy of slaughter.

At least I get to see the sun rise, thought Chris. Light pierced the cloud cover. The sun cresting the mountains. The glint of sunlight warmed Chris's face.

He closed his eyes.

Gunshots rang out nearby.

Chris opened his eyes.

The she-beast paused. The creatures went quiet. Looking back and forth. Confusion and anticipation gave pause to hundreds. The chieftain's grip loosened ever so slightly. A shudder rippled through the horde. Cries and screams. The chieftain growled to a lieutenant.

More gunshots, followed by roars and shouts getting

closer. The one-eyed giant waded through the crowd. It roared and pointed northward. Chaos erupted. Creatures ran in every direction. Grabbing weapons and moving into position.

The chieftain dropped Chris. It roared to its followers, urging them forward. It drew his weapons. The she-beast and other females retreated. The horde seemed to move on a dime, but it was too late.

Engines roared. Gunshots and explosions ripped through the crowd. Monsters sent flying in pillars of fire. The air went fuzzy for an instant. Everything went silent. The dawn air crackled. A beam of radiant blue light hit the one-eyed giant. Blackened flesh and smoke erupted from its chest.

It touched its chest, confused.

Another beam blasted off its arm. Crashing to the ground like a felled tree.

It groaned as it teetered backwards. Creatures screamed, trying to run for cover. Many were too bunched up by the crowd. Unable to run. The giant's body fell. The ground shook. Many screams were suddenly silenced.

Chris crawled into the nook under the broken statue.

An engine roared passed. Chris couldn't believe what he saw. A huge low-riding motorcycle zoomed by. Yellow plating splattered with blood. The rider wore armour, metal armour, like a knight. His face hidden by a huge domed helmet. He swerved, crunching several small creatures under the wheels and chassis.

More motorcycles slammed into the horde. Lances piercing the throats of larger monsters. A squad of soldiers charged, guns blazing and swords clanging. More explosions ripped up the cobblestone. Monsters fell to the ground, their heads blown off by snipers.

A blue-armoured soldier raised a launcher to his shoulder. With an electric crackle, a beam of incandescent light vaporised the top half of a bull creature. Its cauterized waist and legs crumpled to the ground.

Chris saw the chieftain roar at the yellow knight. The knight revved his engine and charged. His opponent, the star-horned chieftain, tried to jump away. Tried with swing with his sword and axe. A huge lance impaled the beast through the chest.

The chieftain died screaming.

Chris covered his ears and hid. Everything was noise and anger. He did what was smartest. *Stanley would be proud.* If he charged out there, he would be killed in the chaos. He was naked. Injured. He clutched his wounded arm. Holding the gash shut. He needed to wait. *Breathe. Just breathe.*

It was so loud. The screams, the bleats, the roar of engines, the crackle of firearms, and the screech of metal against metal.

◆

It felt like an eternity before it went quiet.

He got up.

Chris looked out across the square. The horde had been slaughtered or chased back into the mountains. Bodies piled as high as they were in the festival parking lot. The blood pooled inches deep. Everywhere limbs, heads, organs, and crushed brains.

Knights in various colours walked amongst the bodies. They slayed the remaining wounded monsters with brutal efficiency. Devoid of mercy. Beams of dawn light broke against their blood-slicked armour. Multi-coloured sentinels in a wasteland of bodies.

Where were Curt and Lucas?

Chris walked, then ran, then stumbled to where he thought their bodies were. Lucas and Curt. He didn't notice the knights shouting at him. He turned monster bodies over. He shoved aside the bodies of a few survivors he found. He was on his knees in the blood and guts. Digging. Digging until his nails broke. Stinging pain climbed up his fingers.

"Need to find them. Need to find them!" He needed to find their bodies. He needed to bring them home. Yes. He could find them. "Where are they?" He whipped around, screaming at the knights who stood over him. "Where are they?!"

He saw his reflection in their gleaming armour. He was covered in blood. His hair matted. His body bruised, cut and scraped in dozens of places. His bandages and underwear soiled to the colour of excrement. His cheeks sunken into hollows. His little brown eyes were barely flecks.

He trembled.

The yellow knight kneeled. "It's okay. It's okay. You're safe now." He said in a garbled voice. Chris didn't move. The knight undid a latch on his helmet. Long golden locks tumbled out from beneath.

The knight smiled. She was beautiful. Some would say her eyes were too far apart, or the scar on her eyebrow was too rough. She was stunning. Her face and hair wet with sweat and grime, but her blue eyes were soft. The morning sun dazzled off her armour and golden hair.

She extended a gloved hand. "Come on."

He took it.

♦

Back at the knights' camp, he was given a cup of coffee.

It was warm and bitter. He drank it just to bring life back to his body. The yellow knight wrapped a blanket around him. They sat on the back of an armoured truck. He held the cup to keep his hands from shaking.

A red knight approached, hand on his sword. His dark face looked sympathetic. As did the yellow knight's. The red knight coughed. "Will you tell us what happened?"

"You're not police or army…"

The red knight smiled. "No." He kneeled. "We are not. You've… you've joined our world, young man. You have just experienced a Mass Exposure. Those monsters, they make sport of bringing people into our world and slaughtering them. We've been hunting that group for months. We knew they were planning something. We… We didn't know what was going to happen. We didn't move fast enough." He glanced at the yellow knight. "We are sorry. We failed. We failed you."

The yellow knight held Chris's hand. "You can never go back to where you were from or to what you were." Chris didn't know what to say. After the last twenty-four hours, he'd believe anything. "Just start from the beginning. What happened?"

Chris breathed. "Alright."

SALVAGE

The battlefield was a ruin. About thirty years prior, there was an epic clash amongst Anglo Warlords. Backwater vassals of Dunwich, who were left to sort out their own conflicts until they killed each other off. Whether the battle was over a woman, land claims, treasure, or some half-slight, no one cared to remember.

The stranger stepped out of the dense forest. A huge boulder on her left, the guts of a broken dune buggy scattered around its base. Her face was hidden by her dark hood, her black cloak wrapped tightly around her shoulders. Her hand rested on her holster.

The mists dissipated around her, revealing the battlefield.

A football field of boulders and dead war machines stretched out before her. Rust and moss had long eaten away at much of the graveyard with scattered craters filled in with weeds. Old off-road trucks and converted muscle cars with armoured plates and ramming spikes welded to their chassis. Poles swayed in the wind with the ragged remains of sun-bleached battle standards.

She walked into the graveyard, passing a skeleton half buried in moss. Its head topped with a spiked M1 helmet. An old repeater rusted away in his lap.

The stranger's eyes wandered across the ruins, searching. Her employer had instructed her to find any valuables hidden amongst the metal corpses. He warned her to be careful but failed to tell her why.

Her footsteps echoed across the battlefield. Her eyes straining to penetrate the mists.

Two huge battlewagons were smashed together. A deadly embrace of galvanized metal. A skeleton lay stretched out on the ground, picked clean by scavengers. The iron monstrosities were topped with rusted machine gun pulpits and poles topped with explosive cylinders. *Boomsticks. Stupid name for something fucking dangerous.*

The stranger circled the mountain of metal. Something clanged overhead. One of the cylinder-topped poles fell from the wagon.

The stranger, wide-eyed, dove out of the way.

When the cylinder struck the ground, there was

a mechanical click before the explosion. The stranger shielded herself as the explosion threw her back. Dirt clods clattered against her cloak. She groaned, sitting up. The crater smoked, easily four feet wide and two feet deep in the center.

She glanced around. There were dozens of the explosives across the battlefield. Sticking out of vehicles on precariously leaning poles. Probably more hidden throughout the weeds and grass.

The stranger watched each step forward carefully. Her cloak trailed behind her.

She paused, avoiding an explosive in the ground. She circled around the mountain of vehicles. A skeleton with a spear through his chest sat in the driver's seat of a buggy.

An old Cadillac's grill of spikes bit into the side of an armoured Charger. The stranger climbed up the pile of vehicles. Watching each step and movement with delicate care.

She stood in the carriage of and old Ford when she found a pair of skeletons. Both had died with their swords in the other. Medals on their rotted uniforms, silver boot caps, and helmets with green-bronze horns. One had a snarling battle mask with the face of a bulldog.

The pair of forgotten fools had died for whatever reason.

It must have been real important to them at the time, thought the stranger. She looked out at the vehicle graveyard. All that metal, fuel, and vehicles for this? Those things were rare and expensive on this side of the Veil. Only the wealthy could afford technology like this. *What could have been so important?*

She searched farther into the pile. *I guess it doesn't matter in the end.*

Then she found what she was looking for.

An old Charger. Buried with its stained, grey windows still intact. Hidden from the elements. She climbed through the vehicles until she reached the door. She hung over a crevasse between vehicles. She drew knife and smashed the window with the hilt.

She yelped, almost falling between the vehicles.

A sunken-faced corpse stared up at her with hollow eyes. His armoured spaulders were emblazoned with the snarling face of a hound. A pistol in his hand and a corresponding hole in the side of his head. *Poor bastard must have been completely trapped.*

The stranger opened the door. The corpse's rotten fragrance stung her nose. She cut the corpse out and hauled him out, letting him fall between the vehicles.

Inside, the dashboard remained. Dusty and splattered

with black blood. She got into the passenger's seat, tense for the moment the vehicle groaned around her. She took her knife and a screwdriver and began working the '80s retro-futurist console. She slowly removed the cassette player, the 8-track, orange circuit boards, and bits of useful components. She slipped each into her bag. In the glovebox she found a box of old cassettes. She even took the gold chain and charms off the rearview mirror.

The Earl or Baron or Duke or whatever had tricked out his vehicles with all the toys money could buy. *How many peasant hours had paid for this?* She wondered if they ever got a chance to use these.

She grunted as she slipped from the vehicle with her bag heavy with scavenged pieces. She climbed down the mountain of vehicles and stepped back onto the ground. She flipped through the cassettes as she walked away.

"Nice... Nice!" There were original releases of Beatles, Jovi, Springsteen. "Holy shit." She held up an original Jimi Hendrix. *Now that's cool.*

Her dad would have appreciated it. She hadn't thought about him in a long time. His smiling big eyes. He always fought to make sure she had time for herself from the wall-to-wall studying her mother demanded. *I guess none of that mattered either... None of it does in the end.*

Something clicked under her boot.

Her eyes went wide. Her entire body tensed, waiting for the explosion. After an eternity long pause, she realized nothing happened. She put the cassettes away before kneeling to see how fucked she was.

Her boot had hit the pin of some other explosive. It hadn't exploded on contact and she couldn't hear the clicking of a timer. Whatever it was, it would likely explode the instant she released the pressure.

She sighed. "I should ask for double..." she pulled out her knife. "This can't get any worse..."

Metal clattered across the graveyard. Something alive was moving. A deep musk floated though the mist, followed closely by a snorting-panting sound.

A huge, dark form stepped into view. Hunched shoulders and powerful limbs covered in black fur. A hound the size of a bear. It lumbered past a Volkswagen Beetle and knocked the vehicle over with a grunt. A maw of slavering jowls lined with tusk-sized teeth. Its tiny eyes dulled blue with cataracts. Its wide, dripping nose snorted.

The stranger looked up at the grey sky. *Did I accidentally kick a dog when I was six? Is this punishment? If it is, I'm sorry.*

The hound snorted. It walked clumsily towards the stranger. Its senses were dulled but not absent. The stranger picked up a rock and lobbed it hard.

The clatter sent the hound lumbering in another direction.

The stranger crouched and dug with her knife. She carved up dirt until the cylindrical explosive was exposed. Based on the clatter of metal echoing in the distance, the hound was rummaging somewhere through the graveyard.

Sweat dripped down the stranger's face. She held her breath as she dislodged the explosive, while also keeping her foot pressed on the pin. Her legs began to cramp. She licked her lips as she slowly replaced the pressure from her foot with her thumb. Her hand strained to match the pressure. The cylinder was a tin can covered in dirt.

She slowly stood up. She exhaled as the pain dissipated from her legs.

When she looked up, she bit back a scream. Her eyes met the dull eyes of the giant hound. It stood on the other side of a ruined vehicle. Its heavy laboured panting sending jets of hot rotten air against the stranger's face, gusting her black hair. Its hungry jowls dripped with saliva.

She knew it saw her, so she tried her luck.

"Hi there, big guy!" she squealed. "Who's a good boy?! Who's a good boy?!"

The hound barked, a fresh gust of hot breath hit her face. His hunger overtook his memories of human companionship. He pounced, his heavy body trying to climb over the vehicle. Claws cleaved through metal. The vehicle crumpled under the weight. His massive jaws snapped. The stranger fell backwards, still clutching the explosive.

The hound roared as its heavy body scrambled over the car.

"Sorry, big guy," said the stranger before she whipped the device as hard as she could and bolted.

The blast from the explosion knocked her off her feet, sending her sprawling. She felt the heat on her back. When the ringing subsided, and she heard the violent roars of pain, she scrambled to her feet and kept running. She ran as hard as she could out of the forgotten battlefield.

The stranger vanished into the forest, her black cloak flaring behind her.

♦

The stranger walked down the forest paths back towards town. "If I get sent to another shit show like that, I'm gonna fucking kill him." Her employer would buy her scavenged pieces, and in return she got food, shelter, and a little money. It was a good deal.

Her boots crunched on the dirt trail. The sounds of the forest all around her. There was still the heavy moisture of spring in the air and the migratory birds had returned. The forest was deafening with chirping insects and birds, the wind rustling against the trees and the rummaging of nearby wildlife.

The stranger followed the trail to a split in the road. She turned towards Penn Valley, but stopped when she heard footsteps approaching.

The other person had already seen her. Another woman. A woman alone on the road? *What does that idiot think she's doing?* thought the stranger. *Who am I to judge?*

"Hi there, where ya headed?" said the woman. An Anglo with sunburnt cheeks and chestnut hair around her shoulders and a cap on her head. A smile spread across her wide, pretty face. She carried a backpack and wore a gun belt and holster. A machete strapped to her pack.

The stranger had her hand on her holster, eyes narrowed and suspicious.

"Oh, sorry." The woman held out a hand. "Name's Alys. With a Y and an S."

The stranger kept walking. Alys followed her. "Hope ya don't mind. I'm headed that way. Might be better. Ya know, two women on the road is better than being alone."

The stranger continued walking. Alys followed, a grin on her face.

"So, where you from?" asked Alys. The stranger didn't answer, she just kept walking. The faster she walked the sooner this would be over. "I'm from Toronto, been a while. Don't think I'll ever see it again."

The stranger turned. "I'm from Toronto."

"No kidding?" said Alys. "How long has it been?"

"Almost six years."

"Jesus, really?" Alys looked her up and down. "Does it ever get any easier?"

"Not really," said the stranger. "How'd it happen for you?"

"Monster attack. I was camping along Lake Huron. The campgrounds were attacked by these goat-things. I don't know what they're called."

"Teutonic BrayVolk," said the stranger. "They're just people. Some go into raiding, some are pagan fanatics, some not."

Alys nodded as they walked. "You?"

"Raid."

"By who?"

The stranger paused. Her hand rested on her sword. The silver hilt was in the image of wolves leaping from a tear drop. The blade of mysterious metal, black and unreflective. They all carried similar blades.

"I don't know," she admitted.

"It's a bigger world."

"How long for you?" asked the stranger, as they continued down the trail.

"Two years," said Alys. "I've gotten some help. Just doing odd jobs. People like us are usually in high demand."

"It's shocking how much isn't known here."

"What's shocking is that Dunwich can't set up a public school system, or a train, or anything modern."

"From what I hear, it's the noble houses," said the stranger. "They fight over any issue to retain their own control. They keep seeing our world as a threat to their power—or a way to ensure it."

"Had much run in with them?"

The stranger didn't answer. The bounty on her head was enough. Plenty of people wanted to see her hang. "It's real brave walking from town to town," she finally said. "Most people just find a place and stay there."

"We grew up knowing everything about the world at the tips of our fingers," said Alys. "I don't want to live a peasant's existence now that there is so much of the world

I don't know. You hear that there are huge kingdoms in Africa, like crazy super-advanced ones? Russia is full of giants and mammoths? The Rockies are one massive underground city ruled by goblins?"

"Yeah, I know. I think it's just called the Underground. It sounds like hell."

"But it's modern!" said Alys. "It's like home, with cars and lights and running water. You could find an average old job and get an apartment."

"What did you do? You know, before?" asked the stranger.

"I was still in school, track and field scholarship. I think that's been the only thing that kept me alive until I got some help. You?"

"School teacher," said the stranger. *It truly feels like lifetime ago, or rather, someone else's life.*

Alys looked the stranger up and down again. With her heavy black cloak, longsword and Colt .45 revolver, the stranger looked like death incarnate. She had a rugged beauty to her, but she cultivated her image to terrify people. It was safer.

"It's a wild world," said Alys.

"Yeah."

They came to a split in the road flanked by blooming tea trees. An old wooden signpost showed Penn Valley to the east and Harwick to the north. The stranger's employer was a technician in Penn Valley.

"I leave here," said the stranger. "Good luck, Alys, wherever you end up." She held out her hand.

The girl shook it with a smile. "You too."

The stranger was about to turn to leave when she saw a bead of sweat climb down the girl's neck. Her eyes were dilated.

"You're not going anywhere," said Alys, her smile growing fiendish.

Of course... thought the stranger.

Alys raised her 9mm before the stranger had a chance to react. "Come on. You're coming with me."

◆

"Fucking bitch," grumbled the stranger, as she bit down on a piece of cloth, pulling the knot tight around her forearm. She had several more scrapes and cuts. The worst was on her arm and shoulder. She knew she would need to clean and sharpen her sword tonight.

With bounty hunters sniffing her out, she wouldn't be able to stay much longer. Maybe not even until the end of the week. She needed the money. *Pak had better pay for these.*

She cleared the treeline at the foot of an enormous rock formation. A massive shard of bedrock reaching upwards from the forest. The trail led downwards through a series of pebbly switchbacks flanked by saplings.

Beyond, deep in the valley, was a mass of brown buildings locked between a stream and another mountainous formation. A wood, steel, and barbed-wire palisade locked the town into a corner. Between the rock formations was the blackened carcass of the old coal mine.

Penn Valley. The town was a maze of narrow alleys and crime-infested dens. It stunk of fumes and danger. A dark tumor in the lush green valley, the farming patches and town runoff was like an infection. When the coal mine ran out and people forgot the town, nature reclaimed the hills and crime took the rest.

The stranger walked down the path, boots crunching on the trail. She had been hiding in Penn Valley for a fortnight. She had needed a place to hide since her escape from the asylum at Matslock. At first, she was just drinking in bars and sleeping in an alley she had marked out for herself…

On her third night, her money ran out.

She drank in an old repurposed warehouse, the rafters

still stained black with coal dust. The darkened room scattered with rogues and traitors hiding from the king's government. No one in Penn Valley wanted to be found. Men, women, and others hidden beneath hoods and hats dipped to conceal their faces.

Her head rested against the bar, her cloak wrapped around her. A tin cup of whiskey sat in front of her.

A mercenary with a grey soot-stained beard sat down at the bar. She watched him through the haze. A traveling Franco bard sat in the corner with a guitar and a harmonica. The smooth blues tune gave what little life the den needed.

The old mercenary pulled an inhaler from his vest pocket. He pressed it to his cracked lips and inhaled. The device hissed and sputtered. When he exhaled, a tongue of blue flames poured from his mouth. It didn't burn him. In fact, his eyes dilated, and his shoulders relaxed. The beast of a man seemed more than content as the smell of rotten eggs wafted around him.

The barkeep stepped up to the stranger. A lime-green orc with a broken tusk and a golden ear tag. His shirt, vest, and tie stretched across his heavily muscled chest. His sunken skull-like face frowned.

"Pay your tab, human," he said.

"Just one more," said the stranger with a slurred voice.

"You'll get one more when you pay." He stared down at her with wolfish yellow eyes. His snarl told her she wouldn't be getting out of this easy.

The stranger, through her drunken haze, reached into her pocket and found herself light on cash. *Shit*. She sheepishly set the remaining few coins on the table.

"That it?"

"'Fraid so."

The orc snapped his clawed fingers. Two of the patrons stood up. A broad-chested, red-haired Marklander in one corner. The other corner, a wyrboar, an ugly piggish creature with a snorting face and thick grey arms. Its bristly paunch covered by a tank top.

Before the stranger could draw her weapons, they were already on her. Arms pinned and slammed against the bar. The Marklander patted her down. The stranger grunted, trying to throw them off.

"Holy shite," said the Marklander with an accent. It wasn't Celtic and it certainly wasn't Anglo, more like a slurred sing-song mix.

He set her gun and knife on the bar. As he searched, he left his hands on her ass a lot longer than was comfortable. She ground her teeth trying to resist the wyrboar.

"She's got nothing, boss," said the Marklander. He pulled her sword, looking up at the chalky black blade and shimmering silver handle.

"Fucking human," growled the orc barkeep. "Take her outside, give her whatever treatment you mammals give each other." The orc didn't seem to understand what that meant, and he probably didn't care. He waved them off.

The wyrboar held her up. A jagged grin grew across the Marklander's face. He held her sword in hand. The point merely an inch from his face. He grabbed her chin. His flushed face pressed inches form hers. "Oh, she's a pretty one. Some sorta Sian?"

Sian, a weird bastardized term in this world for Asian.

"And you're some sorta jackass."

He frowned and raised his hand. Her hand popped out and knocked the tip of the blade into his eye. He howled, blood spurted. The sword clattered to the ground as he clutched his face. Before the wyrboar could react, she twisted and slammed her elbow into his face.

The bard put a new excited tempo into his tune.

The stranger locked the wyrboar's grip and slammed him into the bar.

"You bitch!" shouted the Marklander.

The stranger grabbed a stool and smashed it over his head. He crumpled to the ground. With the remaining chair leg, she cracked the wyrboar across the face. The creature finally fell backwards, stunned.

The orc vaulted over the bar, kicking the stranger into a table. It broke beneath her. Her chest heaved. The orc loomed over her, a shadowy titan in the haze of the den. She kicked herself back to her feet. The orc threw a punch. Moving like water, she locked his arm and used his momentum to throw him into a table occupied by three men playing cards.

The stranger grabbed her weapons and dashed for the door. An Anglo man with a Warwich Navy tattoo blocked her way, his hand dropping to the cutlass at his side. She smashed the hilt of her sword into his face without skipping a step and bolted out the saloon-style doors.

Before more could chase after her, she vanished into the alleys of Penn Valley. She would have to move somewhere else to spend the night. She might even have to risk somewhere outside the walls. No one went there. She knew one spot outside town, between two boulders. It was small enough that she would be protected from any wild animals or worse.

She hurried down a dark alley. Her hand on her holster. When she was far enough away, she relaxed her pace. A wolf howled in the distance. The jet-black sky was awash in twinkling stars and distant systems. The stranger wondered if she could even see satellites anymore.

A shuffling echoed through the alley.

The stranger halted, her gun slowly slid from the holster. Her eyes scanning from side to side, searching every shadow and corner. The alley was cluttered with debris; forgotten wood piles, broken mining equipment, overflowing tin trash cans.

She glanced over her shoulder. A small figure dashed back into the shadows.

The stranger scanned with the revolver. Her eyes narrowed. A shuffling sound went through the debris, but it was too dark to see. She followed the sound with the long barrel of her gun.

A pair of horns appeared in the darkness.

She fired.

Metal crashed.

The stranger ran up, a smoking hole was blasted into an old AC unit. She kicked it over and found nothing.

She exhaled. *I'm going crazy.*

When she turned, a huge terrifying bat-like face was inches from hers. She yelped and fell backwards.

When she looked up, she saw an almost three-foot-tall creature step off some debris. Its beady eyes reflected the spotlight moonlight.

"You shot at me!" said the creature in a shrill voice.

"And I'd do it again you little creep! That's what you get for sneaking up on someone!"

"Oh, please. You humans are basically blind and deaf."

The creature walked over to the AC unit. With a knife it broke open the device like a shell. He grumbled and swore as he fiddled with some components. He pulled a battery from his pocket. He strapped a crude device together, creating a low red glow that illuminated the alley.

He wore overalls and a woolen shirt. His squashed face had a flared nose like a bat, along with pale, milk-green skin. His eyes were bright blue, which was bizarre. His bald head wrinkled and liver-spotted with a few stray hairs.

His fingers were the most distracting thing. They were long and spidery, with extremely thin digits ending in small claws. He didn't look like any goblin she had ever seen.

The stranger picked herself up. "I could probably dropkick you over a fence."

"Well, try it, and you'll wake up with a bear trap around your ankle."

"What the fuck do you want, greenie?"

"I *wanted* to offer you a proposition. Then you fucking at shot at me!" he howled.

"Shut up!" barked a voice from a window above.

"Shut your fucking trap, Sally! Mind your business!" snapped the goblin. He looked back at the stranger. "Now, I ain't feeling so generous."

"Fine," said the stranger. She adjusted her cloak and continued down the alley. Footsteps echoing. Annoyed voices grumbled from the windows above.

"Wait, wait," said the goblin. "I'll offer you room and board, even some money. How about that humie?"

The stranger's stomach grumbled. She hadn't even thought about where her next meal was coming from and knew it was far from certain. *Food and money. My two favourite words in the world.*

The goblin grinned with pointed yellow teeth.

"Tell me why," said the stranger. "Plenty of unemployed around here. Why me?"

"I just saw you step out of Anker's with your head intact. More importantly, you're the type less likely to rob me."

"Why is that?"

"Human females don't steal from goblins. They steal

from other humans." The goblin walked past her and turned down another alley. "You coming?"

"How do I know *you* won't rob *me*?"

"'Cause I'm a gremlin alone in the world. No clan. I could use the help." He waved. "Come on. I'll make you some food."

The stranger followed. Her hand resting on her holster.

"What do I call you?" asked the goblin. When the stranger didn't answer he looked her up and down. "Fine. I'll call you Min. I'm Pak. Get it? Pak and Min. Pak-Min. Like the game."

"It's Pac-man."

"Oh, is it? Whatever, name's stuck."

The pair vanished into the misty alleys of Penn Valley.

♦

The door swung open. Min walked into Pak's workshop. Beams of evening light cut through the barred windows. The pale gremlin sat at his workbench with tools and a soldering iron. His blue eyes magnified by a set of goggles to the size of golf balls.

"How'd it go?" he asked.

Min dropped the bag of salvaged materials on the

bench, scattering tools. She headed straight for the mini-fridge and popped a cold beer. *The grandest reward for a bad day, ever.* She collapsed onto the moth-eaten couch. She looked and felt like hell. Covered in cuts and gashes from her altercation in the forest. *Fucking bounty hunters.*

"You coulda mentioned the explosives! And the giant fucking dog!" said Min. She threw back her head and gulped down the cool, fizzy beer.

"You're alive, aren't you?" cackled Pak. "I knew you could do it!" He went through the bag like a demonic child on Christmas morning. "These are good pieces! Peddlers will pay a pretty penny for these."

"Fine, fine. What's for supper?"

"Fish."

"I hope from another valley, I don't want to touch a damn thing in that stream. I'm turning on the TV."

"Whatever you want, Min. You did good."

Min flipped on the small black and white boob-tube. Her week or so of working with Pak was literally the first time in six years she could sit down at the end of the day, watch TV, drink a beer and unwind. It was like falling into a marshmallow. At first, she didn't know how to do it. Now she dreaded that she would have to leave it behind soon.

There were no stations. Just constant recordings of stuff Pak had gotten his hands on. Old creature features, Westerns, '80s swords and sorcery, and even some Kung Fu films with bad dubs. The pair sat in the comfortable silence of the claustrophobic workshop.

Pak worked away on whatever project he had for today. Min drank her beer quietly while Arnold Schwarzenegger as Conan the Barbarian hacked through the head of a giant snake. *Yeah, Arnie? You want to try that for real? Sword is too short.*

Pak's soldering iron hissed as he dabbed at a circuit board.

"You can stay longer, you know," said Pak. "You bring me good stuff."

"Had a run in with bounty hunters today."

"Hmmm…"

"'Hmmm…'?"

"Not a big deal. The Summerset Gang know you're with me. If bounty hunters come in looking for trouble they'll be sorted out with." The Summerset Gang was the local power in town. Mostly just a union of the biggest thugs who owned the most profitable dens and brothels. They kept their court in the rock formations overlooking the town.

"I can't stay."

"I know."

Min sipped her beer. The pain melted away. She let herself enjoy the lethargic haze and Pak's quiet company. *Fucking bounty hunters.* She grit her teeth, trying to move on from the day.

♦

"You guys need better lines," said the stranger.

"What?" said Alys. The bounty hunter aimed her 9mm at the stranger. It had been easy for Alys to take her by surprise. It was elementary. Get her talking, make friends, make her drop her guard.

"It's always the same thing," said the stranger. "'Where do you think you're going?' Or 'Been hunting you for three weeks.' It's never, 'I understand you've had some issues with the law, ma'am. If you come with me, I'm sure we can sort it out with the government.' That would be nice."

"Would it work?"

"No," said the stranger. "It would just be less cliché." Her senses strained. *Two others.* She could smell their sweat and hear their clumsy movements through the foliage.

"Well, then I'm afraid it will have to get ugly," said Alys. "You're going to put down your weapons—"

THE VEILED SAGAS: BLOODIED

The stranger snapped up her revolver and fired. The shot clipped Alys across the neck, blood splattered the blooms of the tree. The stranger ran up and kicked the 9mm away. She twisted around as two others burst from the undergrowth. She hammered the revolver. Two shots took down a heavy-set Anglo man.

Another dove to tackle to her to the ground. She side-stepped from the clumsy attack, flipping him onto his back. Before he realized what had happened, she pointed the gun at his head.

"No! Wait!"

She fired, blood flecked her face.

The stranger turned to Alys, who lay on the ground, clutching her neck. The girl was going to die without immediate medical attention.

"Fuck you," gurgled Alys.

The stranger raised the Colt. The long barrel glinted in the light. She cocked the hammer. Alys glared with unquenchable hate. The stranger saw herself. A lost girl in a dark world, just struggling to survive amongst monsters and magic. She cursed herself for hesitating. A pained smirk creeped across Alys's bloodied face.

A shadow enveloped the trail.

The stranger's eyes went wide. She whipped around. A huge winged shadow slammed into her from above. The revolver was ripped from her hand. Her sleeve was torn. Three claw marks slashed across her forearm. She rolled out of the way, springing to her feet with her sword drawn.

The black blade passed in front of her face as she met her new attacker's eyes.

Above, in the trees, clung a winged harpy. A woman with long, scaly talons, arms covered a feathery fuzz, and a head of scraggly white hair. A simple, belted tunic covered whatever mismatched body she had.

Her hawkish face was set with black, whiteless eyes. In her hand she held a barbed man-catcher. A staff topped with a pair of barbed hooks, like a pair of grabbing arms covered in small spikes.

Not enough to kill, just enough to ruin your day and catch a bounty.

The revolver had clattered twenty feet down the trail. The harpy smiled with crooked yellow teeth. "I guess the bounty is all mine!"

"Whatever."

The stranger ran down the path for her gun. The harpy dove from her perch, talons and man-catcher forming a three-pronged attack. The stranger knocked away the man-catcher but caught another claw-strike on her shoulder. Blood streamed down her arm.

The harpy floated just out of reach, keeping the stranger from diving for her firearm.

I don't have time for this crap. When the harpy went for another dive the stranger dropped and rolled, letting the harpy fly over. When she sprung up, she lobbed her knife she had hidden behind her back. The blade plunged into the base of the wing, just by the shoulder blade.

The harpy shrieked. She crashed to the ground in a furious ball of grey feathers. She was still between the stranger and her gun.

The harpy picked herself up. She narrowed her black eyes and charged, shrieking. The stranger snarled. She caught the hook of the man-catcher on her sword blade. With a twist, she locked the weapons together.

The harpy, carried by her momentum, lost her balance. The stranger slid the blade down the man-catcher, locking the prongs on her silver-crossguard. She pulled the harpy by the neck into the tip of her blade.

The harpy squawked. Her whiteless eyes wide, blood seeping down her tunic. The stranger kicked the body over. The gurgling death rattle whistled from the harpy's split windpipe. A horrible gasp of air until her lungs finally wheezed out.

The stranger collected her revolver, checking the mechanism. The grime and build up would become a hazard, she'd have to clean it soon.

There was a groan behind the stranger. She snapped the chambers shut and fired, executing the remaining hunters. Alys had already bled out, her eyes wide and vacant.

The stranger stared down at the girl, wondering for a moment what her life had been like before she was Exposed. A half-forgotten life in a different world. Two girls from Toronto, thrust into a world of magic and monsters. Forced down a path that sent them hurtling at each other. All that promise, all that potential, thrown into a world that ate promise and potential, leaving only the need to survive.

The stranger continued down the trail.

DUEL OF GIANTS

Within the Rocky Mountains is a labyrinth of tunnels, halls, and caverns, making up a metropolis bigger than anything on Earth. They were originally built by dwarves that came to the New World with the Vikings in the ninth century, but unlike the Vikings, they stayed and built a colonial empire called Nyrvellir.

In the early twentieth century, an influenza pandemic cleared out huge swaths of the Underground Empire. This gave many other families, clans, and factions the opportunity to fill the power vacuum. The most successful of which were the Goblin Clans under the leadership of the Goblin Kings.

Now, millions of people call the Underground home. Or Hell, depending on who you ask.

♦

The elevator rumbled up the shaft. Kelsi hopped

back and forth on her toes. She wore a grey jumpsuit that stretched across her front and sides. A helmet under her arm. A padded gorget kept her neck straight. She tried not to look at her reflection in the metallic walls. She wouldn't let *that* ruin her mood.

Every time she looked in the mirror the words slipped into her brain. *God, I hate the way I look.* She shook her head, forcing the negative thoughts out.

"Someone's excited," grumbled Nik.

"Why shouldn't I be?"

"Not everyone is willing to climb into a giant death machine."

"You designed it! I expect it to be perfectly safe."

"I don't even know how you can be so chipper at..." he looked at his watch. "Two in the morning..." He swore in Dvergr.

"How can you not be? It's been years of work and research! We finally get the big guy to start stomping around! Maybe even swing that cleaver!"

Nik rubbed his eyes. "Your cheer grates on my bitterness."

Nik was a dwarvish engineer, one of the main designers of the Colossi Project. At the behest of the Clan-backed

CorpLords, they were exploring further technological avenues for construction and military technology. His sour face was lined by a short blonde beard pulled into a single braid.

The elevator stopped and the doors slid open.

"Yes!" squealed Kelsi.

The warehouse echoed with the busywork of a dozen different engineers and technicians.

The twelve-foot-tall mechanical platform stood in a metallic frame. Welders reinforced the chassis, sending spouts of sparks around the Colossi's ankles. Coolants hissed from the dozen cables sprouting from the Colossi's back and arms. The red and white metal gave it a terrifying, sports car look.

AtlasOne.

Kelsi ran circles around the big guy, like a child running around a play structure. Kelsi was always going to be the pilot. Nik had been preferred by the bosses, but the team all agreed on Kelsi. Now she could escape the confines of a computer desk to do something truly amazing.

She placed her hand on its knee and looked up at the goliath machine. A grin spread across her round cheeks. "You're gonna be incredible, big guy."

"You know it can't hear you, right?" commented Nik.

"Hush up. You're ruining the moment."

Nik grumbled and headed to the desk where the two goblin technicians, Zvan and Scrik, ran diagnostics. *Two halves of the same brain.*

"How we looking?" called Kelsi, not looking away from AtlasOne.

"Everything is running optimal," replied Nik. "We can get—" There was an electronic chime. He pulled out his cellphone. "God. I got to take this. Start the test without me, otherwise you'll be up my ass to start."

"There are worse places to be," she teased.

He blushed before he ran to the farthest corner of the warehouse to take the call.

Kelsi fought her frown away. He never did tease back. She would have liked that.

"We're all done here," said one of the welders. Teena pulled up her welding mask to reveal her tiny white face. Teena was probably a size zero. Kelsi shoved her insecurity aside. *Not today.*

Kelsi smiled. "Thanks, babe. You excited?!"

Teena shrugged as she pulled off her gloves. "Job is a job is a job. Enjoy the ride, I got a date tonight. I'm going to bed."

"Really?! Who with, the banker or the teacher?"

Teena shrugged. "I think this one is a lawyer, or a collector. No idea, he was complaining about having to get money out of clients."

Kelsi kept her smile. *The girl just keeps picking them until they cheat on her, or vice versa.* It wasn't her place to judge. It wouldn't be kind. "Well, I hope you have a wonderful evening! I'll let you know how the test goes!"

"Whatever," said Teena as she led her team out of the warehouse. All that remained were two other technicians, the goblins behind the computers, Nik, and Kelsi.

Kelsi looked up at the machine and realized that AtlasOne was all hers. She looked at the goblins behind the desk, their green faces illuminated with blue light. They gave her a thumbs-up.

Kelsi grinned.

The goblins pressed the key. The armoured glass cockpit clicked and hissed open. Kelsi climbed in. She ignored the snickering from the goblins as she struggled to get into the cockpit that clearly wasn't built for someone of her build. *Nothing ever is.*

God, why am I so fucking down on myself today? She grit her teeth and pulled the straps over her shoulder. She had to fight to get the last bolt to click. *Well... every day.*

Sure, she had had another bad date last weekend. That was nothing new. Just another guy who thought she'd be easy to get into bed; the mere gift of their masculine presence would force her to spread her legs. Why were they always like that? She sighed. *At least they're willing and have their uses.* But they wouldn't even pay attention when she talked about her work. Top of her class, a PhD with a job that put it to good use, and not one would take interest in her life...

Focus.

"We ready?" she called as she slipped on her helmet.

Zvan and Scrik gave her a thumbs-up and closed the cockpit remotely. The heads-up display appeared against the glass cockpit.

Kelsi's heart began to pound. "Reading me?"

The goblins chirped, "Affirmative."

"First sequence powering up... now." Kelsi flicked the necessary switches at her end while the goblins did their job. A roaring hum rumbled around her. That was why the Colossi was so special. It had an independent power core.

The system hummed with mechanical life.

Kelsi's heart drummed faster, her childlike excitement getting the best of her. The remaining workers pulled away the scaffolds. Now, AtlasOne was under his own weight. The gyros whirled beneath Kelsi's feet, maintaining a constant equilibrium, allowing the Colossi to move on its own.

Kelsi allowed herself the indulgence of her favourite part. With her hands slipped into the control gloves, she raised AtlasOne's hands in front of the cockpit. The huge articulated hands matched hers in perfect sequence. Barely a millisecond delay.

She tested each finger by touching it to her thumb. The precise movements of the Colossi were so organic and natural. Perfect synchronization. Each digit was a skeletal hand padded with plating, wiring, and rubberized pads. Each movement caused pistons in the hand to articulate perfectly. It was hypnotic in its harmonized complexity.

"You ready, Kelsi?" said Zvan with his high-pitched voice.

"Yes, boss." She grinned.

Kelsi had both feet secured in a set of pedals. They locked in her feet and allowed her to control each leg as if it was hers.

With one leg, she took a step, like pumping a bicycle. The Colossi lumbered forward. It didn't lose balance nor crash. No one had to call paramedics for a crushed femur or dislocated shoulder.

Kelsi hadn't realised she was laughing.

The goblins gave her a thumbs-up to continue. The warehouse extended for another two hundred feet. Fabrication stations, lab sections, and other machines along the metal walls.

Kelsi took another step. Then another. Then another. Laughter escaped her mouth and before long she was shrieking with joy with each step.

By the end of the next hour, AtlasOne could march around the facility without being held up by construction cabling or a secondary support. AtlasOne could march on his own accord. Kelsi just loved the control and the power. She wasn't just some *big-boned* girl; she was the first Colossi pilot of the Underground.

"I'm gonna try something," she said over the radio.

She marched AtlasOne to the far side of the warehouse. She flicked some switches to adjust the torque and increase the gyro-stabilization.

"What are you— Oh, no," said Scrik.

Zvan planted his head against the desk. "Alright, fine, Kelsi. Go ahead."

Kelsi grinned and set everything into forward position. AtlasOne lumbered slowly before building speed. He sprinted with earth-quaking footfalls before Kelsi launched both pedals upwards. She felt AtlasOne's feet leave the ground, the gyros kept the equilibrium. He flew ten feet above the ground and thirty feet across.

Kelsi's heart fluttered

The landing was hard, the hoof-like feet held powerful shock absorbers that splayed out for additional balance. AtlasOne hit the ground hard and skidded about ten more feet. The goblins shrieked as Kelsi came to a stop just before their booth.

She grinned. "That. Was. Amazing!" her voice echoed through the radio.

"You're fucking crazy!" howled Scrik.

"You coulda killed us, Kelsi!" screeched Zvan.

Kelsi grinned and stood AtlasOne up straight, fists on his hips. "But did you die?"

The goblins stared up flatly.

"Want to try the cleaver?" giggled Kelsi.

Both goblins slammed their heads against their desk. "Could we stop you even if we tried?" said Zvan.

"Unlikely."

Scrik raised a tiny arm and pointed to one of the

fabrication stations. "Over there, crazy human."

Kelsi squealed and AtlasOne ran over to the third station. On a series of sawhorses rested an eight-foot-long CleaverBlade. A flat ended sword with a rubberized handle big enough for Atlas. The reinforced black steel with a gleaming silver edge.

With those fascinating mechanical hands, she gripped the black hilt. The sword rang when she lifted it. The diagnostics read perfect. She turned back towards the goblins, who were cowering behind their computers.

"What can I smash?!" squealed Kelsi.

"Shut it off! Shut it off!" Nik re-entered the warehouse, waving his arms. "Kelsi! Back to the dock."

"What?" she barked, then realize she forgot to press the radio. "What?! Why?"

"We're shutting the test down. We have to go."

"Why?"

Nik was standing between AtlasOne and the computer terminal. The dwarf wasn't angry or bitter. His face was furrowed in a way Kelsi had never seen.

He's scared.

Kelsi's stomach churned. "What was that phone call about?"

"It doesn't matter. We have to go, now."

Kelsi didn't move. The Colossi hummed around her. Sweat lined her cleavage and sides beneath her jumpsuit. AtlasOne stood with the sword hanging limply in one hand.

"Nik, just tell me."

He swore in Dvergr. "Listen, I just got a call from some associates. Other players, players far above our paygrade, do *not* want AtlasOne functioning yet. I don't know who. I don't know when. We just need to get out of here." He sighed. "This is CorpLord politics and we *need* to leave!"

"And abandon Atlas?!"

Nik sighed. "Yeah."

"We've been building him for four years!" said Kelsi. "I won't abandon him."

"Kelsi, I will not compromise anyone's safety over a machine. We need to leave now."

"Who told you that someone wanted to damage AtlasOne?" Kelsi's voice echoed through the warehouse from AtlasOne's systems. "Some wizard from the Sixteenth District? A jealous orc boss from the Eighth? How do you know they don't just want the warehouse open for someone to come and steal our designs?"

"It doesn't matter. We are not equipped, and our backers

do not have the forces to protect us right now. We're lucky we got this much of a warning!"

"I won't leave."

Nik and Kelsi shared a long look at each other. He was afraid of something but wasn't going to tell her. *Coward.* He was the bitter dwarf who didn't take shit from anyone. How the hell had he been cowed so easily?

Zvan's and Scrik's ears whipped around their heads as they looked from Nik to Kelsi, then to each other. They shrugged and began to work.

Kelsi started to see certain systems shutting down and locking on her. "What are you doing!?"

"We won't die for you to play with a toy," said Scrik.

"We love this thing, but we can rebuild him," said Zvan.

"Not if they come after us. They *know* who's built these. They know who worked on this program! You seriously think that running now will change anything?"

The others looked at each other. Nik didn't have a response, so he ignored the question. "Just shut it down."

Kelsi frowned. This was the one thing she had control over. She couldn't control her biology, her weight, or any of the shit of her life. She could control AtlasOne. She had spent so long on him. She wouldn't let it all go to waste.

Kelsi still had movement; she took a step forward. AtlasOne's hoof slammed against the floor with a huge echoing crash. Scrik slammed the key and Atlas froze in his stance, unable to take the next step.

Another crash echoed through the facility.

Nik and the goblins froze.

That wasn't us.

At the far end of the warehouse echoed another brutal crash. Then another, then another. As it continued, Kelsi realized with horror that someone was knocking on the warehouse door.

Kelsi turned to Nik. "Who called you?!"

"A friend told me someone was coming after us."

The crashes stopped.

"We need to get out of here!" shouted Nik. "Eject her!"

The goblins nodded.

The crashing stopped. Kelsi peered through the corner of the cockpit down the length of the warehouse.

"Eject her!"

Kelsi braced herself.

Before Zvan could press the button, an explosion ripped

the far end of the warehouse. A pillar of flame and twisted metal tumbled down the warehouse. The fluorescent lights running the length of the facility went out, and the red alert lights went on.

In the gaping hole of warped and glowing metal stood a single huge silhouette. A nine-foot-tall shadow with broad shoulders.

"Eject her!"

"Don't!" said Kelsi. "Don't let them win."

The shadow stepped into the warehouse. He carried himself casually with heavy footfalls. Armour ran the length of his arms and legs ending in diamond-shaped shields on his arms and greaves on his legs. The trunk of his body was wrapped in a thick, fur-lined tunic. His face was heavily shadowed in the low, red lighting.

A deep chuckle echoed through the warehouse. He began running, his arms swayed with each stomping stride. Arms ending in vicious-looking punching shields.

Oh, God.

Zvan slammed the keyboard.

Kelsi closed her eyes, bracing for the ejection, but nothing happened except the whirling of the systems returning. The hum of the gyros and the engine around her. Kelsi flexed AtlasOne's fingers. The monster charged, clearing the last twenty feet of the warehouse in two strides.

"Brace!"

AtlasOne raised the CleaverBlade horizontally. The Colossi's joints locked in position, shock absorbers readied. The monster's diamond shields crashed into the blade. Metal scraped against metal, sparks sprayed against the cockpit. In the low light of the warehouse, only the cockpit lights gave Kelsi a proper view of her opponent.

A wide face grit his rotten teeth inches from her cockpit. His shaggy beard was twisted into three braids off his chin. Studs of silver pierced his broken nose and ears. His dark skin was wrinkled and stonelike, as if the face had been cleft from volcanic rock.

He laughed, flecks of saliva sprayed the cockpit

"Nik!" screamed Kelsi over the radio. "Get out of here! Get help!" She wasn't able to glance over her shoulder. *I knew we needed a rearview camera.*

The monster chuckle was like a deep rumbling growl. He used one arm to push down AtlasOne's blade and hammered the cockpit with his other. The diamond-shaped shield struck a small chip off the cockpit's window.

The force sent AtlasOne stumbling backwards. Kelsi tried to stabilize it manually by holding the arms out, but it was too late. The monster launched himself at her with a series of brutal jabs and haymakers, sending Atlas stumbling back farther. She crashed through the goblins' computer station, sending sparks and broken hardware scattering over the floor.

Atlas fell backwards. The CleaverBlade spilled through its fingers and rang against the floor. The force slammed Kelsi's head against the back of her cushioned headrest. The padded gorget and helmet kept her safe.

Out the corner of her eye, Kelsi saw the warehouse's elevator close with Nik and the goblins inside.

The monster stomped forward. He reached behind his back to produce a blowtorch in the shape of a pistol. He grinned and said something in a deep foreign accent. Kelsi didn't understand the language, but she knew the threat.

He flicked on the torch; its jet of blue flame sent ripples through the air.

Kelsi reacted, she pulled her legs to her chest and shot them forwards. Atlas's backwards-bent legs sprung out and struck the monster hard in the chest.

The monster went flying through the air. He slammed into the metal rafters of the warehouse, denting the metal. Fluorescent lights and alert lights exploded into sparks and glass shards. He landed hard against the floor thirty feet away.

Kelsi groaned as she tried to get Atlas upright. *When the hell have we ever had to get him off his back?* When would they have ever even needed to test that? She knew this system, she knew how the hardware and software intermingled into this titan.

Kelsi angled AtlasOne's hips one way and shot her arm forwards. AtlasOne jerked upwards, but not enough to roll. Her helmet hit against the seat again. She threw the arm up again, a little closer to tipping far enough.

The back of her brain already filed this as something to redesign later.

Unless we already did... She searched the keys for something.

She looked down the warehouse. The monster, this giant, the jotunn... she had seen pictures and reports of giants. She shook her head. She had read reports from international magazines. This wasn't just some giant from the North or in mountain valleys. This was a Siberian jotunn. This was a real monster. They, whoever *they* were, sent a mercenary after the Colossi Project. A Siberian jotunn. A frost giant from across the Atlantic. A jotunn warrior from the steppe of Jotunheim.

Her opponent slowly got to his hands and knees. He spat a glob of blood and a single blackened tooth clacked against the ground. He looked up; his eyes were completely black. Not quite like a shark and far wilder. He hated Kelsi even more now.

Kelsi tried to roll over again but couldn't tip the balance.

There has to be something!

The jotunn was on his feet, a little woozy, but anger compensated. He rose and moved to attack.

Kelsi forced the panic from her mind and acted. She shut off the gyros and inverted the arm controls. Suddenly, Atlas's arms flung back and raised the titan back to a sitting position. Kelsi's arms held forward sent the arms backwards in a mirrored position.

She flipped the arms back into standard position just as the jotunn reached her. The arms flung forward. The jotunn hadn't expected it, and both fists came crashing down on his head.

The jotunn stumbled into one of the fabrication stations, sending equipment cascading across the floor.

He growled and swore in VolgaJotunn.

Kelsi had to get out of here. She knew there was a guard outpost across the highway in the next ward. They would be able to help her, unless the entirety of the Seventeenth District had abandoned them to their fates. *God, please keep the others safe.*

Kelsi hit the gyros back into gear and got Atlas to his feet. She had to run. She threw the controls forward and ran.

The jotunn charged again.

Kelsi saw his attack coming this time. She had to use his own aggression against him. That's something Dad would have been proud of. She adjusted the central torque to twist and threw the jotunn into the wall. His charge gave her all the force she needed.

He crashed against the corrugated steel wall, imprinting his figure in the metal.

Kelsi ran without looking back. She lowered one arm, the fingers scraping against the concrete. The CleaverBlade's handle fell into the hand. Atlas crashed through the smoking hole at the end of the warehouse.

The facility was at the edge of an industrial ward. The Colossi Program needed the technicians and materials the ForgeHouses and Fabricators had in abundance. Above Kelsi was the cavern ceiling of the Underground. Lights from other factories bathed the rock in dancing shadows.

In the distance, across ten blocks of flat-roofed factories, Kelsi saw the huge aqueduct-shaped highway arching over the buildings. On the other side, near a PillarTower would be the guard post. The PillarTower rose up like a metal and concrete tree, with roots and branches holding the hollowed mountain together. A dazzling skyscraper trapped within a mountain.

A roar echoed behind her.

Kelsi threw AtlasOne forward. *Not today. I won't let you take my work from me.* Sword in hand, AtlasOne stomped through the parking lot. Kelsi couldn't bother being careful. She clipped Nik's red sedan. *Pay him back later.*

AtlasOne crashed through a wire fence. Kelsi had no way of looking behind her to check her pursuer.

The Colossi ran between two ForgeHouses. The alley was lined with garbage bins and smoking tables. The alley took Kelsi in the wrong direction, she spun Atlas to the side and slid on his hooves. Clods of asphalt sprung around Atlas's ankles.

Kelsi looked down the next alley, towards the highway. Out of the corner of her eye, she saw a shadow barrel towards her. Kelsi lurched within the cockpit. AtlasOne shuddered as he was slammed into the concrete ForgeHouse.

The jotunn roared. She could barely see him but felt him pushing her into the crumbling wall. He locked the arm that held the CleaverBlade. She reached around with her free arm and grabbed his shoulder. The pistons in Atlas's hands fired and the hand clamped on with two hundred pounds per square inch. She felt the jotunn's calcium-hardened bones groan under the pressure. He cursed.

She threw him into a dumpster. He stumbled and used the crumpled dumpster to steady himself. He roared, spitting saliva. His hair in long, rope-like braids lashed with leather and bone.

Someone hired him to do this.

"Who sent you?!" she roared over the intercom.

The jotunn laughed and shouted back in his rough guttural language. She knew they hired him for this very fact. He wouldn't be able to reveal anything without a translator.

"You won't take my work!" She launched into an attack, swinging the CleaverBlade at his head.

The jotunn smiled. He blocked the swing with his shield and dove into an attack. They crashed through the concrete wall of the ForgeHouse. They battled through a bathroom. Toilets and showers already crushed underfoot; spouts of water sprayed Kelsi's cockpit. Lightbulbs and cables sprayed sparks.

Kelsi knew AtlasOne wasn't shielded against the elements yet. He wouldn't survive. She screamed and drove forward into the giant. He reacted fluidly and countered with sharp jabs of diamond shields. More chips in the cockpit window.

Kelsi threw her fist forward, hurtling the sword like a club. It forced the jotunn back. Metal rang against metal. Kelsi used the opening to reverse the pedals and run Atlas backwards into the wall.

She felt the drywall fall behind her like the side of a cardboard box and into the main factory floor.

The jotunn tried to close the distance, but Kelsi kept swinging the CleaverBlade in a wild pattern. He circled her like a wolf, teeth grit. He pounced, jumping off a block-shaped fabricator. He threw a brutal punch against AtlasOne's shoulder. Atlas stumbled back. The gyros were the only thing that kept him standing.

Kelsi pedaled back to gain more room. The jotunn grinned with his rotten teeth. He was enjoying this.

"Oh, fuck you!" barked Kelsi.

They stood in a ForgeHouse. This one was owned by Thorgrim & Co., an appliance and equipment manufacturer. These ForgeHouses were centuries old and switched owners on a semi-regular basis. One year, baby bottles; the next year, weapons for international export.

While the lines of conveyor belts and fabrication machines built refrigerators, dishwashers and coffee machines, there were the remains of the original dwarvish forges. Huge pillar-like chimneys rose up in the main floor, ringed with furnaces with gaping wyrm maws.

This floor led to an industrial bridge going up to a new floor. With the high ceilings, there was a lot of unused airspace. Now new floors were added; more surface area to use.

Kelsi gripped the sword with both hands. The problem with Atlas's design was when the arms held something in front, it made it hard for the operator to see. *Will have to adjust this somehow.* She could see the jotunn's excited grin.

He's faster and just as strong. The jotunn had complete control of his body and a lifetime of coordination. How could Kelsi hope to beat him? She could barely navigate her own body in day-to-day life. How could she possible do this with a mech she had only had a few minutes test? How could she win against those odds?

Everything that could have been thrown against her had been. Genetics that made it impossible to lose weight, shitty guy after shitty guy, and now someone wanted to take away everything she had fought to build.

No. I won't let anyone else take advantage of me. No one would ever make her feel less than ever again and no one would take what's hers. "I'll just have to be smarter than him."

The bridge. She chopped the blade towards his shoulder. He blocked it and jabbed his shield at the cockpit. The force jerked her back. She pedaled Atlas backwards, retreating slowly towards the bridge.

Kelsi swung the blade and the jotunn blocked and countered. It was some kind of game. He threw his jabs with such patient precision. He laughed. The chips in the cockpit grew into cracks. As if a boxer was hammering his awkward, but far larger, opponent.

Kelsi drew him onto the bridge. The industrial grating groaned under their weight. Each clumsy swing gave him more confidence to throw more jabs at her. Kelsi grit her teeth each time he hit. Without the helmet and gorget, her neck would have been broken from the force.

The jotunn scored another hit, this time on Atlas's left shoulder joint. The system reported damage. Kelsi moved the arm and saw that the shoulder couldn't rotate upwards at a 30-degree angle.

"You're breaking him!" she yelled and swung the blade downwards with all the might of the Colossi.

The jotunn blocked with both arms; he went to one knee under the force. The sound of the blow rang through the factory. Kelsi threw the damaged arm and punched the jotunn across the face.

The jotunn's head jerked back, dark blood poured from his mouth and nose. He laughed and said something Kelsi didn't understand. He threw off the CleaverBlade and charged. He hammered against AtlasOne's front chassis. Kelsi shook within the cockpit. She pedaled AtlasOne back. The cracks in the windshield only grew.

Sweat and blood dripped from the jotunn's face. He roared and threw a final heavy haymaker. The air whistled when it landed. Atlas shuddered; its systems were reporting more damage to the arms and rotating midsection.

The bridge swayed under the weight of their battle.

Kelsi's heart pounded in her ears. She was soaked within her jumpsuit and helmet. The jotunn's chest heaved. Gusts of steam shot from his mouth.

"Come on!" barked Kelsi. She raised one arm and gestured to continue.

He grinned and laughed before launching into another attack.

Kelsi got him.

She raised the blade with the undamaged arm as if to attack. He raised his arm to block.

Kelsi grinned. He saw her expression through the window and looked confused. It was too late. She dropped the arm and swept the blade through the bridge. Cleaving through the upper layers of industrial grating like butter, sparks spraying off metal.

The bridge crumpled and the jotunn lost his footing. He fell to his knees to keep his balance as the bridge swayed under their weight. Kelsi swung it again, cleaving further. The entire structure shuddered. The jotunn roared, trying to leap towards Kelsi.

She slammed the flat of her blade across his face. He tumbled to the side, catching himself on the rail of the bridge. The weight was too much, and the scaffolding and rebar below snapped. It crumpled, falling ten feet before jerking to a stop. The jotunn looked up, eyes full of fury as he held on.

Kelsi felt the bridge shudder beneath her feet. She saluted the jotunn. "Good luck, kid."

The jotunn roared.

The bridge collapsed, falling down towards the deeper reaches of the factory.

Kelsi didn't have time to see what happened to her opponent. She could feel AtlasOne becoming unstable. The bridge was about to give out on her too. Kelsi spun

AtlasOne on his hooves and bounded up the bridge. Bits of metal fell around her feet.

She heaved AtlasOne's arms and legs, firing the pistons in his ankles as the bridge fell beneath. "Come on!"

Kelsi threw her arms into the motion, forcing AtlasOne forward. She slammed the secondary systems off and the gyros into overdrive. "Come on, you hunk of junk!"

The scaffolds fell out beneath her.

Kelsi held her breath. AtlasOne launched off the pistons of his legs. Flying through the air, Kelsi reached out with one huge mechanical arm. Rubberized fingertips reaching for the edge of the platform.

The fingers missed by mere inches.

AtlasOne's chassis slammed into the scaffolding below. Kelsi's helmet slammed against the seat. Metal screeching and crumpling, sparks flying. There was nothing beneath to catch the titan. Kelsi felt herself rise in the seat as they freefell through the air. Metal and cabling raining around them.

Kelsi closed her eyes as weightlessness took her.

♦

Kelsi jerked awake. She had no idea how long it had been or how far she had fallen. Some of these factories went deep into the impossible depths of the Underground. Either the old mine or some lower floor. It was hard to tell.

Kelsi blinked. Her head throbbed, and her mouth tasted of blood. The cockpit was a bubble of stuffy hot air. When her vision adjusted, she saw that AtlasOne's arms were thrown forward, protecting the cockpit from the beams and slabs of steel. The cockpit was webbed with cracks; a few shards of glass had fallen around her.

It was dark with AtlasOne's systems down. The red lights of the factory above weren't even visible.

Kelsi groaned, she spat a glob of blood before checking herself for injures. None of the glass had cut through her jumpsuit too badly. She patted at her face, clumsy from the shock and exhaustion, before pulling off her helmet. When she turned it over, she saw it had a dent. She peeled off the gorget too. The whiplash was a mercy compared to a broken neck.

"Fuck," she groaned. Everything hurt. She brushed her sweat-soaked hair out of the way and looked through the cockpit window. She was in the low darkness of a factory floor. The destruction from her battle above had turned the floor into a junkyard of broken steel.

Kelsi wasn't going to just sit there and wait. She flicked on AtlasOne's systems, but nothing happened, which was what she expected. She tried rebooting the system but received no power. She shook her head. "I'll have to do it manually."

She slipped her fingers slowly from the articulated gauntlet arm before she unlatched her boots from the foot pedals. Finally, she threw back the harness. The release on her chest made her gasp. Sweat stained her in all the embarrassing ways she could imagine, but at least she was alive.

She used the emergency latch to open the cockpit. They had planned for a few redundancies. Atlas's arms were frozen in the forward position they had crashed in. Kelsi didn't remember throwing the arms forward in the fall. Maybe she did, involuntarily.

The cockpit was caught halfway between the arms, and Kelsi refused to move them. It was a risk moving at all. Something could come crashing down. Her knees cracked as she stood up on the seat.

I just need to get to the top of the chassis, she told herself. She reached up to climb out of the cockpit. She knew she couldn't lift herself straight out of the cockpit, so she used her legs to shimmy herself out. She had already begun to sweat again... All the useless hours at the gym that barely kept her weight under control. No matter the hours of exercise or diet, her body just wouldn't cooperate.

Nothing would cooperate.

Nothing was going to work out.

She got her head and chest out of the cockpit. "Thank you, Mom, for not letting me join dance because you didn't want those girls to bully me." She grunted, scrambling herself further out of the cockpit. "They were bullying me anyways, at least I'd have been able to dance. Could have proved them all wrong. All of them."

Maybe then I wouldn't have had to go to prom with my cousin. Maybe then I wouldn't have had to put out every time just to keep a guy around. Kelsi growled. "Maybe I wouldn't hate myself so much."

She had her chest out of the cockpit when she heard a crash of metal somewhere in the darkness. A deep low sigh from an alien voice.

The jotunn was somewhere down here.

I'm going to die here.

Kelsi couldn't see where he was, or even if he was aware of where she was.

She bit her lip. *No, I am not.* She could either go back into AtlasOne and hide and hope to God he didn't find her, or she could get AtlasOne working and give herself a fighting chance to survive. She just needed to get across the highway.

Someone must have heard this racket. Someone should have been on their way already. *Unless...* Kelsi's eyes danced through the darkness of metal and factory equipment. Red lights flickered in the reaches above her. *Unless the District really had abandoned them to their fate.* Nik and the others might already be dead.

Kelsi bit back the gasp as she struggled to hold herself up. The throbbing in her head and neck compounded.

I am not giving up now. I can still fight, and I'm going to.

Kelsi's arm shot out and she gripped a handhold on the top of the Colossi's chassis. They had installed these kinds of latches and handholds for easier maintenance. Some of their design choices had had the forethought she needed right now.

She gripped the handhold with one hand, then the other. Her foot slipped and she was holding on with her entire weight trying to drag her back down. *Not this time, you fat piece of shit.* She pulled, biting hard on her lip to keep from yelling.

She slowly got herself out of the cockpit. She lay for a second on the AtlasOne's damaged shoulder. The galvanized metal jabbing into her back. She gasped for air. *Hard part done.* She crawled slowly towards the crown of AtlasOne's chassis.

She tried to avoid the broken rebar and metal scaffolding scattered around AtlasOne like a warped bird's nest.

Deep breathing echoed in the darkness. She had to work fast.

She leaned over the side of the chassis, glancing around for the jotunn before dropping to the ground. She landed hard, biting her tongue. Blood filled her mouth.

Another groan echoed throughout the factory floor.

Kelsi wiped the blood from her lip as she got to her feet. Around her were upturned machines and metal beams, a jungle of steel and metal with nothing but the echoing breathing of a monster surrounding her through the darkness.

She unlatched the power core, which was cold to the touch. *How long was I unconscious?* She was a mechanical engineer; it was the magically-informed technicians who handled the power core. It was impossible technology. Magically enhanced technology. She threw open the core, barely able to see into the opening.

Kelsi couldn't use a light even if she had one. She would have to rely on her memory of Nik's plans. She breathed slowly before reaching into the power core. Residual warmth tickled her knuckles. They must have been down here for hours. That didn't bode well for her chances that anyone would come looking for her.

Jumpstart the power, she remembered. They had redundancy systems to help with that if external power sources were unavailable. She just needed to reach farther into the core for the… Her hand brushed something jagged and retreated immediately. She sucked the blood off the back of her hand.

Damage, of course. Kelsi got on her knees and felt around the back of Atlas. A hunk of rebar pierced sideways through his back. Most of the back plating was warped and dented. She gave the rebar a cursory tug, but it refused to budge. Kelsi got on her back and braced her feet against the chassis. She used her sleeves to grip the rust-layered rebar.

She breathed again, listening for movement from the jotunn. With a sharp pull, she ripped the rebar from AtlasOne. It released easier than she expected, and the rebar flew from her hands and clattered against some distant metal equipment.

Her chest jumped into her throat. She held her breath, but there was silence.

Kelsi scrambled into action; she reached into the power core. Then felt the switch and pulled it, uncoupling the system for the reset. Beneath a grey plate were three push-switches and a flat, grey switch. She pushed all three prepping the entire system for the reset, then pulled the grey switch hard.

It didn't click. The power didn't reset.

A pained groan echoed through the darkness.

Kelsi bit her lip and pulled the grey one again.

Metal clattered.

Kelsi pulled the grey one again.

A confused voice drifted across the factory floor.

Kelsi slammed the switch, it connected. The power core erupted with blue light and energy. The entire system roared back to life. Lights from AtlasOne bathed the factory floor in light. Over the Colossi's shoulder Kelsi saw a figure sitting up in the debris.

The jotunn winced and blinked, raising his arm to shield himself from the light. Hunks of rebar stuck out of his arm, leg, and shoulders. He was bleeding down his face and soiled tunic.

When he realized what the light was, his face furrowed and roared an indecipherable threat.

Kelsi didn't waste time. She scrambled up the chassis, shoving metal beams aside. She looked up; the jotunn was on his feet, swimming his way through the tidal wave of debris and metal.

Kelsi shoved a beam aside, but another piece of metal fell and struck her in the head. She rubbed the growing goose egg. She blinked through the pain as the jotunn closed the distance. She dropped into the illuminated cockpit. Her hands danced across the consoles, resetting the systems and sending everything into overdrive.

The jotunn clambered through the metal. He was almost on top of her.

Kelsi slipped her feet into the pedals.

The jotunn stumbled as he climbed over Atlas's legs.

Kelsi got one hand in the controls.

The jotunn raised both arms with those diamond-shaped shields.

Kelsi got the other hand in the controls and activated the systems.

The jotunn brought his fists down.

Kelsi shot out her arms, catching the armoured limbs in Atlas's huge hands. The servos screeched beneath the titan's plating.

The jotunn roared.

Kelsi smiled and squeezed her grip. He roared, trying to overcome AtlasOne's mechanical strength. She smiled and threw him back, the pistons and gyros screeched. The jotunn flew through the air before crashing into a stone pillar.

Kelsi got Atlas to his feet. The Colossi sputtered and groaned getting up. The gyros sputtered but held the machine's equilibrium. Atlas was damaged. His arms, legs, and power core, sparks of blue energy poured from his back. Kelsi feared how much longer the cockpit would protect her.

She had a choice. *Die or survive.* She was done having no control.

Before the jotunn could recover, she threw AtlasOne forward. She had to find help.

She pedaled as hard and as fast as she could. Atlas limped on his damaged legs. A roar echoing behind her. At the end of the factory floor was an industrial elevator.

Footfalls pursued behind her.

Kelsi threw AtlasOne against the elevator, slamming through the cage and into the shaft. *Let's hope this works.* She grabbed the cables with a vice-like grip. She kicked forward and got a footing against the shaft wall, then kicked forward the other leg. The damaged arm couldn't reach as high, but it was working. Her stomach turned. Gravity pinned her into the chair. With rapid jerking movements, Kelsi got Atlas climbing the elevator shaft.

Kelsi could hear the jotunn's alien threats below her and the scraping of his own climb.

She doubled her speed, metal crunching with each jerky lift. The terrifying routine went on for almost a hundred feet. Sweat beaded down Kelsi's face as she mimed each desperate motion.

At the next floor available, she punched her fist through the door and gripped the floor. She dug the Colossi's fingers in, peeling back layers of white linoleum. She let go of the cable and dug into the floor with both arms. Climbing, clawing, and kicking, she managed to get AtlasOne's chassis onto the next level. From Kelsi's point of view, she was just staring at the flooring, hoping the cockpit wouldn't shatter under its own weight.

AtlasOne jerked back with a weight on his ankle.

The jotunn roared. He slammed his shield into Atlas's knee. A damage signal blared in the cockpit.

She felt a sharp jerk, pulling her backwards into the shaft. Kelsi kicked backwards, it connected with something. A howling scream fell down the shaft.

Kelsi clambered Atlas onto to the level, crumbling a section of the floor as she did. Ceiling tiles shattered off Atlas's chassis as she stood up. She turned the titan around and glanced down the shaft, gripping the elevator door.

The jotunn was alive, grunting as he climbed the elevator shaft.

Kelsi turned away, the adrenaline forcing her forward. She just needed to cross the highway. She crashed through another bathroom—drywall and a burst pipe sprayed the chassis—before she found the lobby. She charged through the glass doorway. Shards scattered across the asphalt as a foreman exited his car for the morning shift. He screamed.

Kelsi pedaled forward, but AtlasOne lost his balance. He fell to one knee. The damage had been too much. AtlasOne was falling to pieces around her.

She looked up and behind her. Pillars of smoke rose out from the factory. Sirens wailed nearby. Someone must have been on their way by now.

Gripping a nearby delivery truck, she forced AtlasOne to his feet. The roof of the vehicle crumbled in her hand. She locked his damaged leg into position, essentially creating a peg leg to limp on.

Kelsi sighed and tapped the radio. "Is anyone out there? Repeat. Is anyone out there?!" She smacked the radio, making Atlas gesticulate comically. "Is anyone out there!? Nik!"

A voice cracked, "Receiving AtlasOne. We lost you in the commotion. What is your location?"

"Who is this?" demanded Kelsi.

"District authorities. We have been searching for you."

"And the path of destruction didn't clue you in?!" Something wasn't right here. Kelsi turned her head. She could hear the sirens from fire trucks, but they weren't heading in her direction.

A vehicle turned down the alley between factories. A black SUV. Kelsi stood AtlasOne up.

The SUV swerved. The door swung open. She saw three men in black suits empty out. Each carried a barrel-like weapon with a cylinder of canisters. Grenade launchers. They hoisted the weapons, aiming for Kelsi.

"Fuck!" She threw Atlas forward, crashing through the cement wall. The launchers popped and explosions rippled through factory. Bubbles of fire sent shards of debris ricocheting off AtlasOne's dented plating.

AtlasOne limped through a factory floor lined with conveyor belts. The wall exploded with more grenades.

"Why is everyone trying to kill me?!"

Kelsi grit her teeth and swerved, skidding the war machine on the cement floor. She charged through the wall, cement cascading around her. An explosion burst at her side, jerking her in the cockpit. It had been a mistake to remove her helmet and gorget, but it was too late now.

She charged the men. AtlasOne's uneven steps crunching against the asphalt. One fired the launcher, an explosion burst against Atlas's shoulder. The arm went dead. She dropkicked the SUV, sending it tumbling into the next building. She swatted two men before they could launch another grenade. She didn't care if she'd killed them or not.

The third, she grabbed in Atlas's huge grip. The launcher fell to the ground. He growled, trying to wriggle out of Atlas's grip. She raised him to the level of the cockpit.

"Who are you!? Why is this happening!?" screamed Kelsi through the cracked window.

He growled. "I'm not saying shit!"

She shook him from side to side like a rag doll. "Say again!?"

He vomited down his front. He was pale, with a short blonde mohawk. His black uniform was soiled. His blue eyes hazed. "We were paid!" he cried. "When the jotunn attacks, we follow. We make sure the robot is broken. We destroy it and the pilot. Scrub the entire Colossi program."

"Why?!"

"I don't fucking know!"

She brought him closer to the cockpit. He could see her control of the machine. She squeezed her grip, the pistons hissed. "Say again?!"

He gasped for air. "Fine! It's just corporate jealousy! That's it!"

"All this?!"

"I think so! They didn't tell me much." He sobbed. "Please! Put me down!"

A roar echoed down the alley. Kelsi turned to find the jotunn standing in the dust of the broken lobby; he clutched his side. His black eyes narrowed and focused.

Kelsi knew AtlasOne couldn't handle anymore. The machine was too badly damaged. The jotunn was hurt too, but it wouldn't make a difference.

Kelsi dropped the mercenary and ran. Atlas limped on. Above the next block of factories was the highway. Along the railing she saw camera flashes from a gathered crowd. She could see the nearest turnpike, heading up to the highway.

She made a break for it. The jotunn roared curses as he pursued.

AtlasOne climbed up the ramp and onto the highway, crashing through a tollbooth. It exploded with glass and sparks as she crushed it underfoot. As she ascended the highway, she looked back towards the factory sector.

Pillars of smoke and bursts of fire scattered through the sector. Her ears twitched. Through the sirens and explosions, she heard gunfire. There was fighting? Was there was a battle beyond her duel with the jotunn?

Kelsi groaned. Her body still ached. She moved towards the next ward. The District Police had to know about this. They must have been battling... someone. The corporate rivals? Power politics between CorpLords, District Kings, and Clan Bosses? Someone had it out for the District, or even just this sector of factories. It was a warzone. A battle between CorpLords and their technologic patrons. Kelsi was a pawn in someone else's game.

The jotunn limped in pursuit towards her. His face dripping with dark blood as he tried to catch her. He swore curses in his language, promises of what he'd do to her when he caught her.

It was a slow, pathetic half-pursuit.

Up ahead was a line of black SUVs and barricades. Red and blue lights flashed on their tops. Men in black fedoras, uniforms, and coats lined the barricades with machine guns.

Kelsi looked back and forth between the jotunn and the

line of vehicles.

Kelsi felt her strength leave her. Her resolve was replaced with defeat. AtlasOne slunk to its haunches, leaning against the rail of the turnpike. She didn't know if she'd be shot or not. What if her side lost? Whichever side that was? AtlasOne was shattered. The systems blared. Pieces broke off with each step until he finally collapsed against the turnpike.

A voice echoed from the barricade line, "Leave the vehicle and come out with your hands up!"

Kelsi sighed, feeling the defeat and failure wash down her throat like cold water. It hurt. She felt the pain in her chest as she kept the tears from flowing down her cheeks.

A squad of men with stun pikes and rifles surrounded the jotunn. He hissed Siberian curses, trying to swat them away. They jabbed the pikes into the spaces of his armour with an electric buzz. He collapsed on to the road. His face slammed into the pavement, drooling.

A pair of men in uniforms stepped up to AtlasOne. Kelsi unlocked the cockpit and raised her arms. They placed her under arrest. Kelsi was shoved to the ground as they handcuffed her. She grit her teeth to hold back the tears. She saw a man in the barricade.

A man with a thin moustache and three claw marks across his cheek.

He looked familiar.

♦

They brought Kelsi to an interrogation room. Her hands chained to the table. Her brown hair hung around her sweaty face. She felt like shit, but she was alive. *I don't know for how long, though.*

Why does it matter?

What would she be leaving behind? Her work? Destroyed. Not many friends. Family was all gone. No boyfriend. Just a string of guys who treated her like shit. Now her work was gone. Now everything was gone.

She sighed and smiled to herself. *But I fought, and I fought hard. I made them hurt for it. I've made sure they'll remember me.*

The door swung open, and the man she saw in the barricade entered. He wore a crisp worker's uniform and carried a case file under his arm.

He had a triangle-shaped face the colour of coffee with three claw marks across his cheek. Kelsi looked him up and down. His boots were muddy, and his knuckles had cuts and scrapes not unlike a metal worker, but his clothes were too clean. He carried himself in a way differently from the factory workers.

He smiled. "May I sit?" A hint of an accent in his voice.

Kelsi didn't say anything, and he didn't wait for her answer. He sat down and opened the file. She recognized the documents and schematics from her own firm. These were the designs of the Colossi. Her destroyed AtlasOne.

"These work well, eh?" he said. "Kept you alive."

"Who are you?"

"Tell me, what improvements do you need on the Colossi's designs? You clearly went through a lot, there must be limitations to the design that you noticed?"

He was too well-spoken to be another factory worker, or even a foreman. He was a boss. Someone with clout.

Kelsi didn't say a word. She sat awkwardly in her chair, feeling herself spill sideways out of it. It didn't matter.

He leaned back thoughtfully for a moment. "Okay, let's clear the air." He reached over and unlocked her handcuffs. Kelsi rubbed her wrists.

"You are safe, Kelsi. You are safe, the Colossi is being repaired. The fucking mercenary jotunn is under arrest and will be tried. Right now, I'm trying to keep the Jotunheim embassy from extraditing the bastard."

"Who the fuck are you?!"

"My name is Pedro. You don't recognize me, do you?"

She cocked her head before a wave of images flashed in her addled brain. She was apolitical, focused on her work, but she knew the District's overlord when she saw him. A District King. A vassal of the Goblin King. Pedro Torres. The Last King. A dramatic title.

He smiled pleasantly.

Kelsi's eyes went wide. "You… You're the District's King. I'm sorry. I didn't…"

"Recognize me? Ha!" he laughed. "You've been through a lot. I funded your project and I personally warned your associates when I got word of a move against us. I didn't have a chance to rally a counterattack before the jotunn hit. Then there were other attacks and the efforts to find you were limited."

"Where are Nik and the others?!" She slammed her hands on the table.

The door flung open and a man with a gun entered.

"Its fine," said Pedro. "We're fine. Bring us some coffee, and… You gotta be hungry, Kelsi? What can we get you?"

"Not. Hungry."

"Come on, kid," he said. "We make a mean Cubano."

That did sound good. She nodded, reluctantly. The man shut the door.

"What do you want?" Kelsi remembered she was a part of this District whether she liked it or not. "My King."

"Hush up about the *My King* bullshit, I want to know if you're still willing to work on the Colossi project?"

"I…" She blinked. "Of course, I am."

"Good!" He smiled. "Now, tell me what would help these designs. While it's still fresh in your mind."

Kelsi looked at the documents, then up at the King. The scars along his jaw had healed but had yet to fade. They were recent. He smiled as genuinely as a person could. His teeth were very white. His wide smile showed them off.

"A rearview camera to start with…"

♦

After an extended discussion, a cup of coffee and the best ham and cheese sandwich that Kelsi had ever had, she was released and free to go home to rest. She had a week to recover and was ordered to call a therapist. Afterwards, she would report directly to the King.

She walked through the metallic hallways of the King's PillarTower. The biggest one she had ever seen. There was a vehicle waiting for her in the parkade to take her home. She crossed a clerks' floor, passing cubicles of adepts and bureaucrats.

Her body ached to every fiber from her battle. Her knuckles and ankles bled from chafing in the suit. She was lined with sweat in every crevice. She felt more disgusting than usual.

No. I don't have to prove anything anymore. Kelsi would be working for the King, directly. She…

Along a line of chairs sat Nik. His clothes were sweat stained, and his beard had become unwoven. He looked up with his blue eyes. He jumped to his feet and ran to Kelsi. "You're okay!"

They hugged, probably for the first time due to their professional relationship. He reeked, but in that good way. He smiled. "I can't believe you did it."

"You waited for me?"

"Of course, I did!"

Kelsi didn't know what came over her. She grabbed the dwarf by the face and pulled him up to hers. Smashing her lips against his. She held him there for a long time, tasting the dust and sweat on his lips.

When they broke the embrace. Nik blinked. "I… uh…"

"I'll see you tomorrow. Pick me up at eight o'clock for either a movie or dinner, depending on how much you want to hear me talk about my fight and our new deal with the King."

Nik shook himself before grinning. "Greco or Nipponi food?"

"Nipponi. I need a massive bowl of noodles." She patted him gently on the face, feeling the scruff of his blonde beard.

She left him stunned before taking the vehicle to her apartment. When she stumbled in, she saw herself in the mirror. She saw the blood, the dirt, the bandages, everything. "I fought a jotunn, lived, and I have a date tomorrow."

She passed out without a second thought, a smile glued to her face.

ATTACK OF THE TERROR

Brightfall was a middling town on the NeoAnglian coast. A fishing village of Anglo and Celtic settlers, grown by Rus and Slav immigrants, and now joined by others from the South. Refugees from Mexica and immigrants from the Carib Republics. All Exposed to this world one way or another. A community of over eight thousand, a town, but not quite a city. The Joyce Family organized and collected taxes for their hierarchical masters. They weren't a lecherous house, but they weren't a paragon of good behavior.

Compared to many other NeoAnglian towns, it was a central hub for traveling peddlers, technicians, and others to gather and barter. A Techfirm from the capital had recently begun construction of a new cellular tower. Modernity would arrive in the community soon.

Most houses had a television by this point, but hardly anyone had real internet access. Rural NeoAnglia was lagging decades behind the capital. The Underground of the Rokki Mountains and the principalities of Franco were modern nations, or as close as the concept could be. NeoAnglia was still struggling to stand on its feet. There were worse places to be, the Yarldoms to the northwest and Markland along the north most coast were backward barbarian kingdoms caught in constant civil strife.

Brightfall was a beautiful destination. A pristine boardwalk with a dozen different restaurants, stunning white beaches, a chateau overlooking the bay from a hill, cheap hotels for travelers.

It had fallen on hard times. Fewer tourists year by year, preferring Franco in peace time with its highly cultured urban centers. The fleet of fishermen who fed Brightfall with their daily catch had been on years of reduced quotas and fuel taxes. Many lived on their boats, in floating houses, or in cramped apartments stacked along the shore side. Grumbling third or fourth generation fishermen with wind-burnt faces and leathery hands.

It was a decent place as far as these things went. Hostile to the outside and change, but fiercely loyal to each other, those they would regard as family. It was a home. They could survive anything.

The night was warm, bristling with the fresh smells of summer.

A clutch of teenagers sat around a bonfire at Widow's Point. Through a Clairtone 7980 Radio, heavy melancholic surfer rock echoed across the shoal. The radio host called the song "Farewell to Monster Island" by Daikaiju. Some music he had received, probably stolen, from someone recently Exposed.

Above the group whirled the lighthouse. Its beam of light illuminating distant cresting waves. Old Man Colhoun was asleep at his post with a clay pipe between his cracked lips.

A ripple in the water went unnoticed by everyone.

On a rock near the water sat Isabel Romas in a blue bikini top and denim shorts. Her dark mahogany hair hung around her shoulders in curls. Her light brown skin almost glowed in the firelight. Shadows dancing across her stunning round face.

Colm Durham sat next to her. He passed her a joint of Yarldom Herb, something cheap from the north. It was sour, but it improved her high.

He smiled at her, his rosy cheeks covered in freckles.

Colm was the only son of the local cobbler. He would have a business to inherit. *Plus, he wasn't bad looking either.* They were about to finish the state-mandatory school age. Soon they would have to think about more important things. *Jobs. Marriage. Kids.*

Isabel and her family came from the South when she was little. She didn't remember very well. The only Latin family in town, they ran a restaurant along the boardwalk. Best food in town. Spicy, flavourful, exotic flavours that the town's youth all flocked for.

Colm smiled at Isabel. She wanted to touch his sunburnt freckles and square jaw. His mess of red curls were somehow just perfect. Her swimming vision made it feel like a dream. She wished she wouldn't wake up.

Isabel saw his hand creeping towards hers. She responded by just snatching his. Some boys take too long to make a damn decision. Her dad might disapprove, but they were both Christians. That should be enough. Most of the world were polytheists of one vein or another.

The pair leaned in and kissed. Colm tasted like sweet amber rum. Isabel ran her hands through his curly ginger hair.

"Uh, guys?" called one of the others.

"Busy!"

"No seriously, guys," said their friend, Chase. "What the fuck is that?"

The couple stood up on the rock and peered back towards the town. The entire bay and wharf between them. Widow's Point was a kilometer-long water break that protected the bay. Isabel held back a gasp. Something moved in the bay. Something big. The melancholy surfer rock booming from the stereo only added to the dread.

A ripple in the water grew into a frothing surge. Boats tipped to the side from the waves. Several sailors were woken up by the sudden movement. They were afraid it was an unexpected summer storm. One man with a snow-white beard was thrown from his hammock.

A few dozen people on the boardwalk were enjoying the warm summer night. Eating tacos and pizza out of paper boxes. A child tossed up sand, shrieking with joy.

A jetty exploded into woodchips as the surge broke through the docks. The clap of broken boards broke the serenity of the shore. The rupture managed to catch people's attention.

A shadow rose out of the bay.

The people along the beach watched in horror.

A huge, arrow-shaped head rose out of the shallows along the beach. A crocodilian face with rows of interlocking teeth jutting out of its mouth. Its white sagging front was splotched with black-blue markings.

Its hungry, red eyes searched.

A tourist smoking on a hotel balcony couldn't believe what he was seeing. A handful of people along the boardwalk screamed at the sight. Several ran, many more were frozen with terror.

The monster took a lumbering step forward, much of its body still hidden in the bay. Water spilled over his broad shoulders. Its black-blue back crusted with volcanic scales and spikes. It lumbered forward. Its powerful tree trunk arms ended in ugly webbed claws.

It stumbled onto the beach on its pillar-like legs. Its clawed feet dug into the surf, upturning heaps of sand. Water frothed around its ankles. Its immense tail swung hard, cracking a fishing boat in half. A fisherman screamed as he was thrown from his boat. The clap of the tail echoed across the town.

It was almost sixty feet long from snout to tail.

It craned its huge head, its nose flaring as it searched for a scent. It let out a bloodcurdling roar. Birds scattered. People clapped their hands over their ears at the piercing noise.

It zeroed in on a target. The meat lockers in the kitchens along the boardwalk. It stomped up the beach, sending up clods of sand. People screamed and fled. A mother screamed where her son was. He had been playing at the edge of the boardwalk. The six-year-old boy stood completely entranced by the creature lumbering towards him, a T-Rex toy in his hand.

It rumbled the earth with each step. Its eyes focused on the source of the smells. The cooking grease, the food, the warm blood of the humans. The mother snatched up her son, the plastic toy clacking against wooden boards. The creature walked straight through the boardwalk, sending up a cascade of wooden debris. It roared and barreled straight into the first restaurant.

Isabel Romas and her friends watched with horror. They were frozen. They were just teenagers, little more than children. Half drunk, half high. What could they possibly do?

Isabel knew she couldn't do nothing. She started running back towards town. The kilometer-long water break of boulders, pavement and the occasional tree. Her bare feet slapped against the rock.

The local authorities were just waking up, having been awakened by the ear-splitting roar. The only deputy in the Sheriff's Office jumped to his position. He ran up the stairs to the watch tower and was horrified at the sight he found. Across the few streets and motel blocks, a fire glowed. A huge monster was digging into the boardwalk like a dog into a chicken.

He snapped himself back to attention and began turning the crank on the siren. A high-pitched squeal echoed across the town. His trembling legs felt like jelly.

Most days it was a raid from gangs in the hills. This was different.

The sheriff and the local militia all ran to the office. The roars and crashes echoing a few blocks over. They quickly changed, stumbling through the offices. They grabbed their rifles and shotguns. Rushing through and back out, they threw on vests and steel M1 helmets.

"Go! Go! Go!" shouted the sheriff.

The squad of armed men was joined quickly by the fishermen and other townsfolk with weapons. Many fishermen carried long harpoons and boarding pikes. The mob rushed through the streets as others fled from the destruction.

What was Lord Joyce doing at the time? From his estate at the north end of town, he looked at the chaos and started making phone calls, praying the lines would connect.

The hunched form of the creature was ablaze with firelight. It's monstrous silhouette glowing stark against the night sky. It stood in the wreckage of the boardwalk. Its fang-lined jaws dripping in blood. The pantries, lockers, and fridges cracked open like meaty walnuts.

The sheriff and others halted. Horrified as it snapped its jaws. The body of a restaurant owner fell apart in pieces towards the wreckage. The monster's red eyes full of contemptuous glee.

"Kill this thing!" screamed the sheriff, raising his automatic rifle. "Attack!"

The patter of gunfire roared. Pinpricks of red appeared on the creature's chest. Ribbons of blood streaming down its striped front. It roared, holding up its flabby arm against the gunfire. Chips of blue-black scales fell away. Its armoured back was immune to the gunfire.

It stormed forwards, walking through cement walls, sending debris scattering. A gas line exploded around the beast's waist. It continued, unbothered by the heat.

"Spread out!" roared the sheriff. It was too late.

A thunder crack of the creature's tail sent much of the mob scattering. Bodies and weapons flew through the air. People killed by the sheer impact were sprawled on the street. The creature's tail had slammed through the nearby video rental store. Its glass and neon front shattered, bodies impaled on the debris. The sheriff was one of them.

Surviving fishermen charged forward with pikes and harpoons. A prickly phalanx of desperate townsfolk. The creature was prodded backwards as dozens of thrusts and slashes caused more trails of blood to stream down its front and legs.

It roared, unable to use its tail at the incoming attacks. It swatted with its claws, cleaving the militia into bloody chunks. One man was crushed beneath its feet, reduced to a red smear. Sporadic gunfire resumed and peppered the creature with flashes of searing pain. It roared, overwhelmed by the onslaught.

Isabel curved the end of the water break. Her lungs burning and feet bleeding. Tears streamed down her face. Chase's dad's half-ton sat on the shoulder just off Widow's Point. She jumped through the open window and snagged the keys from the cup holder. She turned the key. After a few desperately long clicks, the engine turned over and roared to life. The dread surfer rock blared over the radio.

In the distance, the monster tore through the defenders. The porcupine of pikes and harpoons forced the creature back. It stumbled through the motel, shattering the building. It dug through the motel like a child walking into a sandcastle. Screams echoed through the cascade of falling debris. It left behind a canyon of destruction.

Isabel slammed on the gas and drove straight back towards town. The earsplitting roar echoing across the bay. Flames and destruction illuminated the monster's bulk. Its immense form stomping through buildings, destroying more of the town. The crack of its tail destroyed the liquor store and killed three more fishermen.

Isabel swerved down the main street. Townsfolk, her neighbours, streamed past the truck, fleeing with their children woken from their beds. From between the storefronts and the surviving side of the hotel came the enormous monster. It loomed over the street, a god of death. An oceanic titan of the kraken-infested depths. It roared and swatted at the gunfire of the militia.

Isabel gripped the wheel with white-knuckled terror. Her face and dark hair sweat-stained and dirty from the smoke. Crocodile jaws snapped, blood dripped from between its teeth.

This is my town, you piece of shit, thought the girl, gritting her teeth. She slammed on the gas.

The truck roared forward. People jumped out of the way. Several fishermen saw what she was doing. They charged forward, stabbing at the creature. It roared, swatting at the pikes. Several more people lashed by its huge tail.

Isabel screamed as the car hurtled towards the monster's tree-trunk sized leg. The truck bucked, knocking the leg out from under the creature's immense bulk. Its top-heavy body fell and crashed through a diner. Glass shattered and the gas line exploded.

Isabel groaned, sitting up straight. Blood streamed from a cut on her forehead. Her neck roared with pain. The front of the truck was crumpled like paper and smoking. She kicked open the dented door and collapsed onto the cement. The slow haunting surfer rock still rumbled over the radio.

The militia moved forward through the destruction towards the monster's motionless body. They crept over the debris cautiously. A younger man in overalls, Sammy Prince, carried an M1 Garand, prowling through the shattered diner.

Just that morning Sammy had gotten his eggs and coffee in the same place that lay destroyed around him. He was just a part-time mechanic and fisherman. What did he know about fighting monsters?

The creature's huge head lay amongst the wreckage. Flames flickered from the destroyed kitchen. Its interlocking jaws shut, eyes closed, and its arm pinned under its bulk.

He crept closer, weapon raised. He gulped and brought the weapon to up shoot it in the eye.

Sammy's sweaty hand threw back the bolt and pushed it forward. When he looked up, the creature's eyes were open. It turned its head, jaws opened to reveal a tunnel of teeth and a barb lined throat.

They snapped shut with the slap of a damp towel.

Its tail cracked, knocking over the half-crumpled truck and smashing through the gathered crowd. Bodies flew. Isabel was almost crushed. She stumbled backwards down the street as the creature recovered and continued its attack. It crawled on all fours like a lizard. When the surviving few militia charged, it opened its blood-drenched jaws wide.

A deep glow erupted from its throat.

A pillar of flame poured from between its teeth, scorching the street and setting six men ablaze. They screamed and waved their arms as their flesh turned black and hair burned away. The creature snapped them up in its jaws, ending their screaming in an instant. Isabel overcame her terror and ran. She ran as hard as she could.

She ran back towards the boardwalk, now completely destroyed and flickering with flames. Pillars of sparks flying up into the night air. Her parents' place, Romas's, was a skeleton of rebar, wood, and plaster. Completely destroyed. Flames climbing up the night sky in ribbons.

Isabel fell to her knees. Her half-naked body bruised and bleeding. Tears dripped down her sweat-streaked face.

The creature knocked over a parked car near the fishmarket. It had its fill and crawled back towards the shore, destroying the empty stalls. It dug it claws into the sand. Its huge form slunk into the water. A sinking boat exploded into driftwood. The shadow of water vanished into the ocean beyond.

The creature would be called the Terror by the survivors. The town of Brightfall burned in its wake.

To be continued in… *The Fleet's Revenge*

Writer. Creator. Geek.

Zachary F. Sigurdson (Z. F. Sigurdson) is a writer from Winnipeg, Manitoba. Born 1995, he graduated from the University of Manitoba in 2017 with a politics degree. Having set aside academic aspirations for creative ones, he has written numerous short stories with several reaching publication.

Interests include reading, writing, schlock moves, fantasy, horror, monsters, dinosaurs and history.

He has worked as a journalist for The Manitoban, as a farmer, as a cook, as a clerk, among other professions.

---

zfsigurdson.com @ZFSigurdson95 zfsigurdson@outlook.com

Made in the USA
Monee, IL
03 July 2021

72839429R00180